Praise for Carol Emshwiller

"Ms. Emshwiller is so gifted . . . "
—*New York Times Book Review*

"First and foremost, Emshwiller is a poet—with a poet's sensibility, precision, and magic. She revels in the sheer taste and sound of words, she infuses them with an extra-ordinary vitality and sense of life."
—*Newsday*

"Emshwiller's readers know her to be a major fabulist, a marvelous magical realist, one of the strongest, most com-plex, most consistently feminist voices in fiction."
—Ursula K. Le Guin

"The most inventive mind in science fiction."
—Karen Joy Fowler, author of *The Jane Austen Book Club*

"Carol's stories turn the corner into another dimension."
—Harlan Ellison

"The woman is a genius, period."
—Gwenda Bond, *Shaken & Stirred*

"Emshwiller consistently pokes holes through the fabrica-tions of our lives and reminds me of the power literature has to change the way we think."
—Pam Harcourt, *Books to Watch Out For*

"Lord what a thankless thing it must be to produce such exquisiteness."
—James Tiptree, Jr., author of *Her Smoke Rose Up Forever*

"Emshwiller's sentences are transparent and elegant at the same time. Her vocabulary, though rich and flexible, is never arcane."
—*The Women's Review of Books*

"Carol Emshwiller stories should come with warning labels: Do not operate heavy machinery while reading these stories. Avoid psychedelics when reading an Emshwiller story. Do not stay up all night, reading story after story by flashlight, under the covers."

—Eileen Gunn, author of *Stable Strategies and Others*

"Carol Emshwiller... has a dedicated cult following and has been an influence on a number of today's top writers.... It is very easy to fall into the rhythm of Emshwiller's poetic and smooth sentences."

—*Review of Contemporary Fiction*

Praise for *I Live With You*

"A collection that manages to remind us of great writers like George Saunders, Grace Paley and Harlan Ellison all at once, though Emshwiller is a unique and wonderful writer in her own right."

—*Time Out*, a Top Ten Book of 2005

"Compassion and a sly sense of humor shape the insight-filled fiction.... Lyrical and resonant ... "

—*Publishers Weekly*

"Her eye for detail and ear for poetry allow her to create compact fables that resonate beyond their immediate settings." —*San Francisco Chronicle*

"Emshwiller's strange, often sad, and beautiful stories linger, unfolding long after reading them."

—*Booklist*

THE
SECRET
CITY

Works by Carol Emshwiller

Novels

Mr. Boots (2005)
The Mount (2002)
Leaping Man Hill (1999)
Ledoyt (1995)
Venus Rising (chapbook, 1992)
Carmen Dog (1990)

Collections

I Live with You (Tachyon, 2005)
Report to the Men's Club and Other Stories (2002)
The Start of the End of It All (1990)
Verging on the Pertinent (1989)
Joy in our Cause (1975)

Awards and Honors for Carol Emshwiller

MacDowell Colony Fellowship (1971)
New York State Creative Artists Public Service grant
    (1975)
National Endowment for the Arts grant (1979)
Pushcart Prize (1987)
New York State Foundation for the Arts grant (1988)
ACCENT/ASCENT fiction prize (1989)
World Fantasy Award for Best Collection (1991)
Gallun Award (1999)
Icon Award (1999)
Nebula Award for Best Short Story (2002)
Philip K. Dick Award (2003)
World Fantasy Award for Lifetime Achievement (2005)
Nebula Award for Best Short Story (2006)

CAROL EMSHWILLER

THE SECRET CITY

TACHYON PUBLICATIONS
San Francisco, California

The Secret City

Copyright © 2007 by Carol Emshwiller

Cover illustration by Ed Emshwiller
Cover design by Ann Monn
Interior design by Alligator Tree Graphics

Tachyon Publications
1459 18th Street #139
San Francisco CA 94107
(415) 285-5615

www.tachyonpublications.com

Series Editor: Jacob Weisman

ISBN 10: 1-892391-44-9
ISBN 13: 978-1-892391-44-5

Printed in the United States of America by Worzalla

First Edition: March 2007

0   9   8   7   6   5   4   3   2   1

To Eve, Susan, and Stoney,
and their spouses,
and to David, too

LORPAS

LOST. IT'S WHAT I WANT AND WISH I WAS AGAIN.
Home is . . . used to be . . . wherever I was. Wherever
I put down my folding cup, wrung out my cap,
turned it inside out and used it for a pillow. But that
was yesterday.

When I was discovered, I panicked. They woke
me out of a sound sleep. I fought. First without
thinking at all, and then because they could be mug-
gers, and after that, when I saw they were policemen, I knew I might be kept in one place and have to
stay with the natives for longer than I could stand.
Someplace with nothing but a little square of sky.
And that's exactly how it is.

They gagged me with a dirty rag. I suppose I was
yelling. They tied my hands behind my back. I
couldn't get a handkerchief for my bloody nose.
They let me bleed all over my shirt.

I did do damage. I don't know how much but they
had bloody noses, too. Maybe a few black eyes.

They washed me, shaved me including my head. I
suppose they were worried about lice. I had a mus-

3

tache. That's gone. I hardly know myself. They did all this with my hands tied behind my back. I calmed myself with breathing. I tried to imagine a sky instead of a ceiling.

I should be glad for the chance to rest, I haven't stopped traveling—not even for a day, but still I long to be moving. They took, not just the laces, but my shoes. I had added two extra heels on one for my bad foot. Even though they're worn out, I'm lost without those particular shoes. That's not the kind of lost I like to be.

I think I'm the last, though I keep hoping there's others of us hiding out somewhere. Mountains would be the most logical place. I was headed there. Mother and Dad implanted their own beacons under our arms, but did all the parents do that and was it the same lumpy red spot for all? And how could I ask somebody, "Lift your arms and let me peer into your armpits?" Even at the beach, I seldom see under anybody's arm. I suppose that's why they put it there in the first place.

I blend in. I never do anything that *they* wouldn't do. I presume we all do that.

We hoped for rescue. We waited. At least Mother did. She never belonged. She was never comfortable here. Most of those of her generation waited and kept on acting as tourists until the money ran out. They thought that would be the best way to survive here until rescue. Unfortunately there was no central location. Now the old ones are all dead and most of the younger ones I knew are spread out, who knows where?

I no longer hope. Actually I never really did. I played Mother's game in front of her . . . the game of wanting more than what we had here—Mother said we were rich back there—but I knew no other life. Actually no other life than poverty. I was used to it. As long as we had enough to eat, I was happy. Besides, I was born here. This is my land. I never look out at it without a thrill. Even as a child I secretly relished this world. I wondered if I'd have to leave if we ever were rescued. Would Mother insist that I go back with her?

Mother said, "We may look more or less like them, but we're not them and don't you ever forget it." She said, "Keep wandering, wear tourist's clothes and carry tourist things." She said, "Just keep waiting. Don't use the freeze, but don't let it die. Don't marry one of them. If you don't marry one of us, it surely will."

I waited. I didn't marry. Now I fear there are no more of us left to marry, though one can't be sure, we were spread all over. And who knows, maybe in some mountain range, some of us might have lasted disguised as campers. There's the rumor of a secret city. I was on my way to try and find it.

They called themselves tourists. Our parents just wanted to see this place for a little while. It was a class in understanding aliens. Mother was one of the guides but empathy was hard for her. She tried but she always hated the natives. "Homo sapiens sapiens," she'd say with a sneer. "Sapiens. That's what *they* think. They took *two* sapiens for themselves, for heaven's sake."

I could never see that much difference, us or them.

Had I known we'd never be rescued, I'd have mated with one of them in spite of Mother's warnings. She was sure I'd reveal myself in a fit of anger, but I don't think so. (Though considering what I just did, maybe I would have if woken up suddenly.) I could have had a normal native life. But could I have asked one of them to follow me, a limping bum in a baseball cap and a flowery Hawaiian shirt, with camera, field glasses? Never lost but always lost? (Though I'd have settled down if I'd married. There must be some way to get an identity and then a decent job.)

After my parents knew we were abandoned here, they went from job to job. Nobody ever got to know us nor we them. Mother didn't want us to know the natives. She didn't want us contaminated. She said we were born for better things than houses with pictures on the walls and malls and coffee shops and grocery stores—better things than little plots of land with flowers in them. . . . Trouble was, that's all we younger ones knew.

At first my family lived in a camper but then had to sell it. Our father got a broken-down pickup truck and a tent and we went from place to place. My parents looked at everything with the same interest they'd had in the beginning, and often laughed at the native's ways, but they always felt set apart. They didn't want to join this world. They homeschooled us so that we knew more about a distant world and its wars and landmasses than we knew of this one.

I TELL THE POLICE MY NAME IS NORTH. NORMAN North. At the time I was looking out the slit of a window that faces North. I don't have papers. I don't know how to get any. I don't ever say my real name. I haven't said it in so long I'd have a hard time pronouncing it. My fingerprints are probably in the network, but not for any crime and not, until now, for any violence. I don't know what came over me. I may be too old for this kind of life.

"What were you doing sleeping in somebody's back yard? Don't you have anyplace to go?"

They're sorry they hit me so hard but, after all, I was hitting them.

"You scared an old lady half to death with your snoring. She thought you were a bear."

I know I look more like a bum than I used to: faded flowery shirt, tan . . . used to be tan pants, used to be fancy shoes with raised heel on left foot.

"Do you have a place to live?

"I want to get up into the mountains."

"Do you have a place to go there?"

"I know people camping up there."

"Who."

"Family. More of us Norths."

"You don't have any camping gear. And look at your shoes. You'll need boots."

And so forth.

I ask, "Am I in for vagrancy?"

"We're going to keep you for a day or two."

When I say, "But I'm a tourist," they laugh.

They not only don't believe me, they don't trust me either. They've left the handcuffs on all this time. I don't blame them. One of the policemen who talks to me has a swollen jaw. I'm lucky he didn't try to get even as they questioned me.

FINALLY THEY TAKE OFF THE HANDCUFFS AND LEAVE me be. I curl up on the bench. There's a dirty blanket. I wrap up in it anyway.

I think of our kind of music. My mother's songs in the homeworld language when she sang me to sleep. What little I knew of my language I've forgotten except for the words she made us memorize from the beginning. Our very first words. I still remember what they mean: "We are the people. We are the tourists left here in hundred eighty-nine. Take me home."

At first we tried to stay in our travel groups, but that got to be too hard when the money ran out and each had a different idea of what the proper thing to do was. That was in the early days. My sister and I were toddlers. If stuck, as we are here, with no other mate, I was supposed to mate with my sister. But she was taken as a mate long ago by one of our others. Mother thought that was best, and that I should find myself another from one of our groups.

So now I sing. Hum. Remember my dead. Wonder if my sister's still alive. I ask for paper and pencil. They say, yes, I wait, but they don't bring any. I suppose I don't deserve it anymore than I deserve better meals.

After a day or two locked up for vagrancy, I'm usually taken to the edge of town and watched as I walk away, but this time I'm kept. I suppose I'm considered dangerous. I find a place on the side of the bench to scratch off the days. I'll have to use my fingernails.

I wonder if my camera, jacket and cap, and my extra shirt are still under that bush on the edge of town or have they brought all that here? If I behave myself will I get them back when . . . *if*, that is, they let me go?

For somebody always on the move, staying still four days is more than I can stand. I always walk as fast as my bad foot allows. Here, I walk to and fro all day. I didn't at first. I lay on the bench until I realized that wasn't doing anything for my depression. Not that depression isn't my usual state. Moving makes me feel like myself. Being a tourist has become my nature.

I yearn for the mountains, not for themselves or their beauty, though that, too, but for the high hidden valleys where you could hide a whole town. (Some say Vilcabamba was never found.) My people would pick a beautiful spot. They loved how beautiful this land was. Before they knew they were stranded here, they talked of wanting to stay forever.

I'm going to get out of jail by any way I can though can I still freeze if I never practiced? Considering none of us were ever allowed to freeze a creature of any sort, I doubt if we could anymore. Our parents always told us we should die before we revealed ourselves because that was a promise they had made before they signed on for the trip. Yet it seems to me some of the creatures here have that same talent.

But we hardly need it. Here on this world with less gravity, we're stronger. I wonder how many I fought that night? I almost won. So far I haven't needed our "save yourself" talent.

THERE'S ONE OF THE GUARDS MORE SYMPATHETIC than the others. He shared his sandwich and his coffee with me.

His name is Smith so they call him Jones and Jonesy. I like their sense of play. I call, "Jonesy."

"You think I've got nothing to do but talk to you? I got paperwork up to here."

"I could help if I had some paper."

"I don't think the chief would want me to give you any. You might kill yourself with the pencil. You rest up. You need to put on a little fat."

An odd thing to say. I'm a wide, heavy man, all my people are, but I guess I look like a too-thin wide heavy man.

"Are they ever going to let me out? You must admit the food isn't the greatest."

"You gave six men a hard time. Now how did you do that?"

"But I didn't win. I'm here aren't I?"

"Were you a boxer? You look like you lift weights."

What to say? I haven't ever been anything.

"Something like that."

"Try to hold out for another day or two. How about I bring you fried chicken?"

So I wait. I pace. Four steps one way, four steps the other. I imagine weeds—rabbitbrush in bloom, bright yellow along the edge of road. That's how it was last I walked. I mark off another day. Jonesy must have said something because the food gets better.

At night everything is lit up bright as day. Another reason to get out of here. Plus there are mice. Bold as could be. I try not to spill anything but they're here anyway. If I did have paper or a book they'd be chewing on that.

The three Fs: Flight, Fight, or Freeze. I hold one of the mice in my stare. He doesn't move. I count to twenty, then I let him go. Or maybe he held *me* and let me go. Or maybe we just stared at each other, one creature to another, and then decided that was enough.

I'M TO GO IN FRONT OF A JUDGE FOR ASSAULT AND vagrancy and goodness knows what else. Finally, Jonesy takes me for a shower. (I've been washing in a basin for five days.) He sits at the door. I want out of here before they dress me in a red jumpsuit and take me off to a bigger, better prison. This is about the biggest jail I can stand.

I washed my flowery shirt and chinos, and I have my shoes back. The day of my trial there's only three men to help me into the van. I won't need to test the freeze. My strength is why I've never needed to try it.

I LOCK THEM IN THE VAN, DRIVE A COUPLE OF blocks, turn off on a side street and ditch the van. I walk a few blocks and hotwire a car. Drive two blocks and pick up another. Walk again. It won't take the owners long to find them.

I'm heading for the place where they first found

me. I want to see if they left any of my things there. It's on the edge of town and on the road towards the mountains. Not hard to find. It's a messy place, that's why I chose it. And next door to other messy places. The house needs paint (as the neighboring houses do) and the porch roof is about to fall down. Best of all there's a big yard full of bushes and weeds—rabbitbrush, black brush, baby tumbleweed, and the big bushy good smelling sage that I slept under. If only I didn't snore like a bear.

I go straight to the sage and check under it. My red jacket with the white stripe along the sleeves is gone and my extra shirt. My little kit with comb and razor, gone. Why didn't they give it back to me in jail? I'll look a mess without it.

I crawl out from under and stand up. I hear a sharp intake of breath. The old woman I scared . . . I presume it's the same one . . . is on the porch looking right at me.

I wonder that she's outside in this heat—someone as old as she looks to be should be inside keeping cool. I can see a swamp cooler on her roof but it's not running.

She sits back down with a plop and then sags over as if in a faint. I should see if she's all right. I should urge her to go inside. But I don't want to scare her again. Of course my head is shaved and my little black mustache gone. Even if she had seen me hauled away she wouldn't recognize me, but I'd scare her even so. Maybe all the more with this shaved head.

I go up to the porch slowly. I can think of some excuse. I could pretend to be selling some religion or other. They're all into religion, especially out in the country, maybe especially those of her age.

I go up the porch steps. I say, "Madam?" but I know that's wrong for around here. I say, "Misses?" Then (oh yes), Ma'am. "Ma'am? Are you all right?"

She isn't. I come closer. I touch her shoulder. Gentle as my touch is, she collapses all the way down. I catch her before she hits the floor. I feel her pulse. I lean to feel her breath. She's alive.

I pick her up and carry her inside. She's small and light, even for one of them. Hunched over from osteoporosis. It's a wonder she didn't break something from her fall. Lucky it was more of a sagging down slowly.

I put her on the couch. The cushion is already lying sideways with a head shaped dent as if she had been napping there not so long ago.

I start the cooler. Then I look for the kitchen so as to find a towel to wet. I also get her a glass of water. Then it occurs to me that maybe I shouldn't wake her up just yet. I put the water beside her and the wet cloth on her head. Then I go to look around. I need men's clothes. And a razor.

The house is much nicer inside than I expected. Not clean, but nice things. And, in the kitchen, all the latest appliances. No sign of a man, though. If a man had been here that first time she'd not have been so frightened and it would have been the man who found me. Come out with a rifle, no doubt, and shot me on the spot.

Still there might have been a husband. She may have men's clothes. Sometimes they keep everything, though sometimes they get rid of everything in a hurry before they have a chance to think. Mother was like that. She got rid of all there was of Dad (not much) and then was sorry later. As was I.

The bedroom is small and cramped, the bed unmade. I suppose she doesn't have much energy for cleaning anymore. There's the picture of a man on the dresser but no men's clothes. She must be one who threw away all her husband's things right away. But when I check more carefully, I find a man's workshirt in with her things. She's probably been wearing it herself.

It's a blue farmer's shirt. I take off my flowery shirt and put on the farmer's shirt. The buttons are a little stressed across my barrel chest and the sleeves are a little short but I roll them up so it doesn't matter. It's so old it'll tear easily.

In the bathroom I find several pink ladies razors. I put a few in my pocket.

As I come back to check on the old lady, I see a man's jacket hanging by the front door. Frayed corduroy, out at the elbows. I've hardly seen a uglier one. Has she been wearing that, too?

There's a whole array of hats on the rifle rack next to the door. Except for one .22 at the top, the rack holds only canes and hats. I find a floppy soft one

with a brim I can pull close over my face. I'm
going to stay away from baseball caps from now
on. I'll be a camper. One of those canes will be nice,
too.

It's a very small house. Even so I wonder if I can
hide here a few days while the police are running
around looking for me. Let the chase simmer down
until they think I'm long gone.

Just as I come back to the living room, the telephone rings. I step behind the door. There's an
answering machine. It's a woman's voice. "Mother, I
can't come up this weekend. Mickey has an ear
thing. The same as he had last time." But then the
old woman staggers up, holds on to the furniture.
Says, "Oops," as she plops into the chair by the
phone. Her hello is breathless.

Now that she's answered, I can only hear her side
of the conversation. "I'm fine. I had a dizzy spell but
I'm all right. I lay down on the couch and I'm much
better now. I'm going to make myself a cup of tea.
I'll stay in here by the cooler. Yes, Rosemary comes
on Mondays and the police are checking with me
every day . . . ever since they found that man in the
bushes."

Doesn't she remember seeing me? Or maybe she
doesn't want to mention it for fear of worrying her
daughter.

I go to the kitchen and put the kettle on. I start
back into the hallway, but she's wobbling there, one
hand on the wall. She goes to lock the front door.

She mutters to herself. "She lets him eat anything he wants. He's not getting enough vitamins. But I've got to keep my mouth shut." She goes down the hall to the back door and locks it, too. Says again, "*Got* to keep my mouth shut."

I stand "stone still" (as we say, not the natives) beside the jacket at the front door. She doesn't see me. I don't think her eyes are very good.

When she comes into the kitchen and sees the kettle already boiling, she says, "I'm even more addled than I thought." Perfect. I'll hide here a few days. I don't think she'll notice and even if she did she'd think she was mistaken.

She gets out a saucer, pours in cream and puts it on the floor. I'm thinking, addled indeed, but then she calls, "Come on kitty, kitty, kitty." It doesn't come. I'm not sure if there is a cat or if there just used to be.

She putters around for a few minutes and I think she's forgotten about the tea. But no, here comes the teacup. She hesitates, puts it back and picks another, puts that back, too, finally settles for the third. These people care about little things of beauty.

I've never lived with any of them. In fact nobody in my family wanted to get that close. Mother was afraid we'd get to be like them, and maybe not mind being here. She wanted us to yearn for the home planet as much as she did. All her life here was nothing but yearning to be some place else. I don't know if all that yearning was worth it. She died looking out over a wheat field. She said, "What is all that gold?"

"Wheat," I said.

"Just like the rivers of home," she said. "Have we gone home?"

I didn't know whether to tell the truth.

"Oh, Lorpas, tell me, are we home at last?"

"Yes, yes."

I don't know if she believed or not.

The old lady sits with her tea and turns on the radio. That's nice for me. I've hardly ever heard their radio or seen their television. Another thing Mother didn't want us to get to like. Before we were born and before they were stuck here, Dad said they had watched and listened to everything they could and raved about how funny and fun these people were. How funny they were especially when they acted almost just like us. But they didn't want us children turning into them. Without home planet experiences they were worried. That was a mistake. It kept us ignorant of everybody and everything here. I had to learn everything after they were gone.

So now I stand still and listen. I hear news but nothing about me having escaped. I hear afternoon thunderstorms are predicted for the next few days. Yes, I'll stay until the weather gets better.

She keeps muttering to herself. Mostly I can't hear but I do hear: "For heaven's sake," and, "Good grief." Then, "More rain. What else is new?" (Odd for the desert, but it's been raining every afternoon.)

She says, "They say doing the crossword puzzle keeps your brains going." Why did she say that? She's not doing a crossword. Then, "Well, lots more than just brains will be lost one of these days. The mountains . . . lost them a long time ago. Bert's house. Barbara. I wish Mother and Dad could have seen the things we have now. They thought things were amazing back in their day. Wish everybody lived together in one village like they used to a hundred years ago. But I always think that same thought. Wonder what use it is thinking the same things over and over." Meanwhile the news is going on and on and she's not listening.

I know how she feels. I have that same wish, too, to be with others like me.

Somebody knocks. She wobbles to the door hanging on to the furniture and walls. She says, "Oops" several times. She left the fire on under the kettle. I don't see how she gets along here by herself. Somebody must check on her every now and then. At least I hope so.

While she's at the door, I step into the kitchen and turn off the stove. I listen.

It's a policeman.

"Ma'am? You all right?"

"I'm fine."

He doesn't say anything about me escaping. I suppose he doesn't want to worry her.

"We'll check 'round later. But don't hesitate to call if you see anything suspicious."

"I will."

"You be sure now."

"I will."

After, she locks the door again. She mutters, "I'm so old I don't suppose it matters one way or the other—what happens to me." Then, "I must remember to water the trees. How long has it been? I can't keep track of anything anymore."

(If she forgets, I'll do it.)

She doesn't finish her tea. She goes back in the living room and lies down on the sofa. Gets up again and brings a fresh glass of water. Lies down. Gets up and turns on tapes for learning French. Lies down and falls asleep.

I make myself a cheese sandwich. I don't drink any of the juice, there's not much left. Not much of anything left.

The cat (there is one) comes out and watches me but won't go near the cream. It's a marmalade tabby. I say, "Hello, Red." She won't come close. I reach to pet her but she backs away. I wonder if she can smell that I'm alien. I've seen dogs go crazy when they get close to one of us—attack or cower. I've always had trouble with dogs. Far as I can tell, cats don't do that.

I search the house again. I examine what must be the daughter's room. It's larger than the old lady's and fancier. There's a new bed and a white dresser. Yellow walls. I'll spend the night in here. I like this sunny yellow.

The old lady keeps on sleeping. I wonder about her supper. There isn't much food around. I wonder if I dare go out and get more. And would I get locked out? I'll unlock a window. One that's hidden in bushes so I can go in and out without being seen. Certainly nobody will expect the escapee to be shopping at the local grocery store. But I'll have to use her money.

She has some good magazines and books. Mother didn't want us to read their things but we managed to anyway. Mother tried to write books for us herself, but she wasn't very good at it. She even illustrated them. Her drawings didn't make me want to live back home though I pretended they did.

"You've never tasted anything like those little ground berries. You've never seen a real sunset. There's moonshine every night. There's no such thing as dark. And sometimes both moons at the same time." She'd always say that last on a particularly beautiful moonlit night. I got tired of hearing it. If I said anything good about life here, she always said, "You're turning out just like them. Besides, you don't know what you're talking about. Someday we'll go home and then you'll see."

I sit in the daughter's room and read. I leave the door slightly open. I skip around from *Discover* magazine, *National Geographic*, and a book on wild flowers of the area. I don't hear her coming until I hear, "Whoops." And then, "Oh, I left the door open. I must be getting curdled. Addled that is."

She shuts the door. I drop down behind the bed with my magazines, but she opens the door again and takes a look around. Says, "The spread is all mussed. Did I leave it that way?"

In she comes to straighten it and sees me, there on the floor. And there she goes, down again. She must have heart trouble. I reach to catch her and keep her from coming down too hard.

I put her on the bed. Then I remember how she forgot me when she woke up that first time, and I carry her into the couch again. I get a cold wet cloth and glass of water again.

But this time she comes to in a few minutes. Sees me, says, "Sam?"

I help her drink. I say, "Yes."

Then she says, "You're not Sam."

"No. I'm Norman. Would you like some more tea? It'll be good for you. You rest. I'll get it."

I make a fresh cup and help her sit up to drink.

"Still dizzy?"

"A little."

"Are you hungry? I'll get you something to eat."

"No, no. I'm fine."

"You should eat. I'll bring you something."

"Who are you? Why are you here?"

"I'm here to help. Let me get you something."

I heat up a can of chicken noodle soup. (There's only one can of soup left.)

Though my taste is probably different, I choose the bowl as carefully as she chose her teacup. When

I come back she looks to be asleep again, but I wake her. I think she should eat.

When I see how she drips all over herself, I feed her. She keeps looking at me . . . not suspiciously, but with curiosity.

"Norman? Who? Where's Rosemary?"

"She'll be here."

I help her to the bedroom. Without me she'd have to hang on to the furniture. I help her on to the bed and take her shoes off, cover her with the small blanket at the foot. "Call me if you need me. I'll be in your daughter's room. I'll keep the door open so I can hear."

I don't want to eat the last of the soup. I eat more cheese and a shriveled apple and go to bed.

In the morning I wake to the sound of the old lady rattling about in the kitchen. What woke me was her loud "Oops." I wonder what she dropped or spilled. But mostly I wonder if she remembers me.

I slept well. Better than in jail with the light shining all night, but I wake hungry. I'm going shopping.

I peek into the kitchen cautiously. I don't want her in a faint again.

"Ma'am? Good morning. Remember me? Norman?"

Thank goodness she does.

"Oh, yes. I felt so much safer all night with you here."

"I'm glad. I need to get us more food. Lock the door behind me and let me in when I get back."

She says, "Take the car. I don't drive anymore," but I think not. It's probably known all over this little town which car is hers and that she never drives it.

I don't tell her I left the daughter's window open just in case. I don't tell her I took some of her money.

I'm wearing her husband's shirt and I put on the floppy hat that will cover my face a bit. There's a small backpack there but it's too distinctive. I'll just have to carry the things home in the plastic bags.

Before I leave I check on the magazines for her name. I might need to know that. Ruth. Ruth Hill.

I GET THREE MORE CANNED SOUPS. I GET A COOKED chicken, eggs, strawberries, (Mother said the berries of our world were better, but I don't believe it when it comes to homegrown strawberries), apples and a few breakfast bars for me for when I take off into the mountains.

When I get back she won't open the door. Says, "I don't know any Norman."

"I brought you groceries. More soup. I said I would. At least open the door and take them in. I'll stay outside."

"That's just a ploy to get in. I'm not stupid."

"Ruth. I made you chicken soup last night. You said you slept better with me here."

"No such thing."

"I've got strawberries, eggs. Ruth. I've got a cooked chicken. You're running out of food."

"Rosemary will bring more on Monday."

It was Monday yesterday. Nobody came.

"It's Tuesday. I'm the one bringing your food now."

"Oh."

But she doesn't open up.

"The police said there was an prowler sleeping in my sagebrush."

"I slept in your daughter's room, remember? I brought you soup and chicken."

"Oh."

Long pause.

"Ruth?"

Just when I'm thinking to go around and in by the window, she opens the door.

SHE WATCHES ME MAKE CHICKEN SANDWICHES FOR lunch and, for her, warm milk with vanilla in it.

It's not too hot yet. I sit her out on the porch so she can watch the quail and ravens. Later I see the cop come. I don't hear what they say. But he leaves.

Later still, when I turn on the cooler and bring her in, she says, "Rosemary reads to me."

"What would you like?"

"Something out of *Discover* magazine. The latest issue is in the living room. We were reading about

Saturn. I do like Saturn. We have binoculars around here somewhere if you'd like to take a look tonight."

"I would."

"I can show you where to look."

She's not like Mother. She likes being here.

It seems Rosemary took her out for walks Monday evenings now and then. Do I dare? Well, I will anyway. She shouldn't sit around all day. When she's alone I'll bet she spends most of her time lying on the couch sleeping to those French tapes.

We go after supper when it cools down. There's several canes by the front door. She picks one. She leads but on the way back she gets lost. Lord knows where we'd have ended up. I warn her never to walk by herself but she insists she'd be fine except she's glad she has me anyway.

So now I've been here six days and nobody has come to help her. Nobody has brought her groceries. I'm wondering about Rosemary and about the old lady's daughter. I don't see how she'll get along without me. I even see some improvement in her awareness in the short time I've been here. I think she's eating better and sleeping better. She's not so shaky. When we walk in the evenings she seems stronger and she usually knows the way home. The cops come and speak to her every day. She always says things are fine. She doesn't mention me. Maybe she suspects something about me but likes me even so.

There's another call from her daughter. They talk

a long time. Mostly it's about her grandchild and mostly the daughter speaks so I don't hear anything but Ruth's answers now and then. She says she's getting along fine. She says she feels better than ever. I'm sure that's true.

We watch TV every night, and I read to her. I'm enjoying myself more than I have since I lost my family. Actually I enjoy living as one of the natives. Also it reminds me of the last days with Mother, though Mother faded away fast and of course didn't dare go to any of their doctors, while this old lady is getting stronger every day and less addled.

One day at breakfast, she looks at me . . . studies me. . . . I see her thinking. (My mustache is coming back. My hair is growing out.) She says, "Who pays you?"

I don't know what to say.

"I don't think anybody does. Where did you come from."

I guess there's nothing for it. This is it. I say, "Jail."

"You escaped."

"Yes."

"You're the one who hid in my yard that first day."

"Yes."

She thinks.

"Is your name really Norman?"

"As much as any other. Actually my mother called me Lorpas."

"Funny name."

But then we spend the day just as usual. The policeman comes to check on her and she says everything is fine.

Later, on our evening walk, holding tight to my elbow, she says, "Norman, I'm glad you're here."

She knows the names of the mountains that loom above the town. She remembers the trails she used to hike and her favorite places up there. She teaches me the names of plants and flowers and birds. If she doesn't know them we look them up in her books. I find her binoculars and we look at stars. She names the constellations. She looks out from her porch and admires the clouds. Every day she checks on her apricot tree and her apple tree. I'm thinking how nice it would have been to have had her as my mother. After all, I'm here, born here, been here all my life, I should have learned about this place and enjoyed it the way she does.

And she's funny. She laughs at being old, at her dowager's hump, and her wrinkled face. She says she used to be six inches taller. That still wouldn't be very tall.

And then they come, my people—to rescue me. They home in on my underarm implant. First I feel the implant as if it's burning me. Then I feel my body buzzing and my whole arm hurts. I don't know how I know, but I know it's them, my people, finally come to rescue us. Finally what mother was waiting for.

They're wearing our usual: bright shirts and base-ball caps, mustaches. . . . There are three. I recognize them right away. They have the tubes to send me home. Mother told me about those little silver tubes that can send you home or burn you depending on the trigger used.

Ruth and I are on the porch. We were watching strange red clouds. No doubt that was them.

They're clearly odd . . . alien. Barrel-chested, as am I.

We stand up and Ruth grabs my elbow. She says, "Who are you people?"

But they haven't bothered to learn our language. They babble out my kind of talk, but I've forgotten everything except the phrase Mother made us mem-orize. But that was: I'm one of the people of one eighty nine, and, take me home.

I'm ashamed of them. They look flabby and pale and ridiculous. How could anyone have taken us for tourists?

Ruth says, "What do you want?"

I move in front of her. I say, "No!"

Two grab me. Ruth pulls me back. They talk but I can't tell what they're saying. Their voices are gut-tural. Mine is, too, but I seldom think about it. Plenty of people here have voices like mine.

Ruth is trying to protect me, as I am her. She's pushing at them. Punching them. We get in each other's way.

They laugh. They don't realize how strong they

are compared to these people and especially compared to an old lady. They pull her away and I hear her arm crack. I hear her cry out.

How can they do that?

I use the freeze. I use it as if I'd always used it—had practiced it on more than just one mouse. As if it was my first instinct instead of what I'd always kept myself from doing.

They pause. It's working. Except I can only hold one at a time. They're laughing again. Even more. I think they'll fall down from laughing.

I go crazy just like Mother was always afraid I'd do. I yell. I fight. I'm in better shape than they are. Also I know how to fight and they don't. I hit and kickbox. I use all the strength I never dared use. As they fall, they disappear, back where they came from I suppose. Except the third one. Before I can get to him, he turns a tube on me and on Ruth. Then he disappears.

I'm burned, but not too badly. Ruth is. . . . I see right away she can't be alive. I suppose they thought . . . I *know* they thought, as Mother would have: It's just one of *them*, she doesn't matter.

Where they stood are three man-shaped clouds. They dissipate quickly.

I carry Ruth inside and put her on the couch. I straighten her arm. She hardly looks like Ruth anymore. I cover her with the afghan she made. The days are hot, but the nights are cold. I touch her burned cheek with my lips. It's not Ruth.

I gather up food into the little backpack that's by the door. I take a poncho. I take a cane. I open the door and let the cat go free. "Come on, Red. We're on our own." She heads for her favorite tree, while I head up the road that goes toward the trail. I'm not lost now. I take Ruth's favorite hike. She said, "Walk up steeply for a mile from the trailhead, and after that there'll be a cliff, pass under it, take the rocky switchbacks up the far side. Soon there'll be a lovely hanging valley with glittery pebbles full of mica. Farther on, cross the stream on the stepping stones, after that, the lake called Long. On the way down the other side, you'll round a corner and it will suddenly open out to a view of snowy mountains all in a row. It'll be so beautiful you'll shout."

THE SECRET CITY

It's high and far and lonely and secret and lost . . . around every corner a blank wall or a cliff, streets that end up against a rock face, or that curve and curve and come back on themselves. Trees grow from the middle of the avenues, and from the roofs of houses. They have to for camouflage. Every wall is covered with vines, every roof collapsed or covered with bushes. There are entrances, tall as three men and wide as six, that lead nowhere, or into narrow hallways that end in cul-de-sacs in which one may find a packrat's nest. Why make it as if thousands of years old, cover it with moss and vines, tumble it into ruins? Why build a park and playground in the center of the city where there's a jungle gym for the children, but one can't tell it from the jungle around it? Even standing right on the main square, you'd not guess there was a city here.

Deer and foxes walk down the streets more often than people and don't know they're streets. Wild goats jump from roof to roof, pediment to pediment, and see no difference here than jumping from their cliffs. Owls hoot all night or scream.

But the animals depicted over the doorways and along the pediments are none of these, they're of a kind never seen on this world. Birds that have no feet and look like fish with wings, feathered creatures with five eyes. There's an animal that's all mouth and hardly any body. There's an animal that looks like a flower but with teeth and six long leafy legs.

All this, not only so the young ones can see something of the world they're missing, but so they can grow up among their own kind and not be contaminated by the natives. Also so they can wait for rescue together and not be scattered over this whole primitive world.

The disadvantages of the city are, it's even more primitive than the natives' world, and you never see the sun except filtered through the leaves. The advantages are, you never feel the full force of hail or sleet of mountain storms and you're hidden so well not even a low flying helicopter would guess the city was here.

ALLUSH

BACK WHEN WE WERE CHILDREN, THE WHOLE CITY was our playground. We still know every crook and cranny. We know where to avoid the bears and wild cats, where to hunt for deer. . . . My favorite spot is where the fox kits play. I sit, not stone still, just normal, moving if I want to, and the kits come right up to me. Mostly from the back. I make sure not to turn around. They don't like to be looked at. Funny, it's the runt that comes up and looks at me from the front. She's the boldest. Or maybe the stupidest. But she's my favorite. I love how they sound like cats and look like them, too. Odd how a canine can seem so much like a cat.

But domestic cats don't last a half hour up here and didn't even last on the way. We brought some with us when we first came. None of us kids wanted to come so our parents brought along our cats and dogs. By the first week out, coyotes got every single one. We'd brought mine. She was a calico. I found her the very first morning of our trek, with her stomach torn out. Why didn't our parents know that would happen? They should have known. I know our world is so much better that they didn't think it was worth while paying attention to this one, but they should have known.

We all thought we'd be gone back to Betasha, the real world, a long time ago. Most of us hate it up here, especially in the winter. It's boring and cold, and there's hardly any of us left anymore. Except I always like playing with animals and climbing trees, but I remember movies and TV and radio and books down there in the Down. Not that we don't have plenty of books. But I remember store-bought clothes and store-bought food—TV dinners all ready to eat. I was only eight when we left, but I could heat up my own supper.

When the old ones got up here they didn't have anything to do—of course they didn't and neither did we—so they built the city. They said, for us children, to show us the marvels of the homeworld but I think they were homesick. I wonder that they bothered, what with everything phony, and everything fake overgrown so it wouldn't be discovered.

Back in the early days here, every now and then they'd go back to the Down to get supplies, but they wouldn't let us kids come with them. They kept the way secret so we couldn't ever leave the Secret City without one of them.

I did try to run away one fall. A long time ago. I tried to get back to the Down before winter came. I was tired of this primitive living. I hiked for three days. I was determined. All I found was more mountains. I had to backtrack on my trail to find my way home.

But in the summer it was fun. We were free. There was no crime. Nothing to fear but falling out of a tree or mountain lions though mostly they kept away from our city. We made pets of whatever was around. Sometimes garter snakes. Sometimes horned toads. And there's my foxes.

Nobody's gone to the Down for a long time now and there's only Mollish of the old ones left to show the way. When she dies, nobody will know how to get back. But that's what the old ones wanted—for us to stay here with the locked-up homing beacons and wait for rescue.

Before we came here and built the city we lived, more or less, with the natives, always in poverty and always waiting to go home. The Secret City is harder and more primitive even than being poor in the Down, but the old ones kept saying, "Can't you stand it for a few years? Rescue *will* come. Our own people would never leave us stranded on such a backward world. As soon as they can, they'll pull us home."

They put all their beacons in a vault in the center of the city, locked up tight. Our people will home in on them and take us back. If we don't stay near, our people won't know how to find us.

Everything is better on our homeworld, the technology more advanced, also the views more beautiful, the flowers, the sky, the birds, the two moons. . . . "Oh, Oh," they said, "the two moons, one blue of ice, one iron-oxide red. Oh, the sun shining on the sky dust. . . ."

But sometimes, when I go out from under the canopy or if I climb a tree all the way to the top, I see a sunrise that's so beautiful I think: What could be better? Even though I know on our world everything is. Everybody says so. I can't wait to get there. I wonder if there will be creatures like foxes and blue jays I can tame.

The old ones thought all these piles of mossy rocks, all these half-standing overgrown walls would make the town harder to find even if approached from the ground. They didn't think about archeologists. So far those are our only. . . . We call it eliminations. They thought they'd found a place a thousand years old and of a civilization never known before. They had a GPS. They were so excited they were shouting. Thank goodness cell phones don't work here in the mountains or they'd have phoned out right away. They were scraping at the lichen and pulling down vines. We didn't have time to think: Wrong or Right. We had to act fast before word got out that the city exists.

Youpas took care of all four of them by himself with bow and arrow. I was afraid of Youpas even before that. I suppose we're all wild up here—how could we not be, but Youpas is the wildest. He left the Down when he was only six. (I was only two years older.) But the old ones all said the natives were way worse than any of us could ever be. They said we were the civilized ones. If the natives are worse than Youpas, that scares me about being in the Down, but I liked life there more than here even though I know there are bad people and bad things that happen there all the time.

Now that we're so few left up here, we don't bother with lookouts anymore. That's how this man sneaked in without us knowing. He could have been here several days before I realized he was among us. That's the disadvantage of a place like this, we can hide out here easily, but so can anybody else.

This man must know how to get back to the Down. I hope he didn't just get lost and end up here by mistake. I wonder if he'd be willing to go back and take me with him or at least show me the way.

I lean close and examine him as he sleeps. How fascinating a whole new person is. I haven't seen somebody else for a long time. Makes me feel, even more, that I want to go back to the Down. Or, actually, anywhere else but here.

I wouldn't be surprised if he wasn't one of us. He has the eyebrow ridges and the barrel chest, the ruddy complexion, the black hair with reddish streaks. But sometimes some of them do look a lot like us. That's why the old ones had no trouble coming here as tourists. I wish I could see if his eyes are that aluminum gray ours always are. I wish. . . . I hope. . . . But . . . well, how could he not be us?

His clothes are machine-made. Only his shoes seem to be of leather but they're finely smoothed. We used to have clothes and shoes like that, but even our hiking boots are worn out by now. His shoes are just regular. They'll be ruined in no time. One of his heels and the sole, too, is raised on one side. He must be lopsided. And he has a cane.

He's been burned across one side of his face. It's raw and blistered. If not for that, he'd be a handsome example of one of us. Of course the natives wouldn't think him handsome, they like a smoother blander face. I used to think as they do, I didn't want to be one of us, but I like his looks. A lot.

I spend the night nearby, he on one side of the wall and I on the other. I listen to him snore. It's like sleeping with a bear. Even though I'm out in the open, I feel safe with that racket going on.

LORPAS

THOUGH I WAS LOOKING FOR IT, THE SECRET CITY was so secret I came upon it inadvertently. I actually spent a night camped within its outskirts before I noticed it.

I had walked for days, always taking the paths less traveled. I was in pain from my burns. Every time I crossed a stream I stopped and wet my burned shoulder and face with icy mountain water. Often I was tempted to stay right there and soak myself until I healed but I wanted to get well away from any natives. This time of year they'd be unlikely to be more than a few days out. The knapsack pulled at my burned shoulder so that it bled, but I kept on.

Once, in a grassy meadow, I followed browse trails by mistake—tracks that went back and forth aimlessly. Then I saw that some of the upper tracks converged into a single path and I followed that, over a high pass and then down into a sheltered valley. The path was difficult, one cliff after another. Sometimes I had to sit down and lower myself over boulders or turn around and crawl down backwards, yet it was a clear path. It looked to be used by elk and bears and such, to go from one valley to another when the seasons changed. Two valleys back, I had walked through a group of elk lying on a snowfield chewing their cud.

When, on the sixth day, I climb up and over yet another high pass and see yet another view of snowy peaks and below them, a cozy valley, several rivers rushing down, I think, If my kind wanted to build their secret town what a perfect, hidden spot. They'd have water and a place where planes couldn't come in low between the cliffs—on one side granite, pink tuff on the other, above that a cone, red with iron oxide, between them an alpine section, with a canopy that not even a low flying helicopter could see under.

But when I finally get down to the valley floor, there's no sign of my kind—or anybody. I'm disappointed. I had this daydream that the rumor of a secret city was true and this was where it had to be.

I wanted to rest up with my own kind, the tourists stranded here. I wanted to be called by my real name for a change, and most of all I wanted somebody to cut away my implant so my kind couldn't find me and try to rescue me again. Now that they've finally found a way to snatch us home, it seems they want us all back and no questions asked.

I'm so tired the moment I'm all the way down into the valley and under the trees, I wrap up in the poncho and drop where I stand.

I dream my people did live here but they, and I also, are all snatched back to our world where we're strangers and none of us can remember the language or the writing. The air is dense and cloudy and tinged with a silvery mist and we have trouble breathing. I wake suffocating—shouting—jump up in a panic. It's dawn. I sit back down on a stone to catch my breath.

It's then I notice the stone I'm sitting on seems to be part of a wall and there's a symbol carved there, weathered away to almost nothing. I've forgotten my own language and writing, but I remember this. It's the syllable *ath*. An entrance marker. My people *have* been here. How can it be they were here so long ago as to have this sign almost completely worn away? Or is the symbol only half carved because my people were snatched home before they could finish it? Were they like me and didn't want to leave?

I follow the wall farther up and see another symbol. This one I've forgotten. The farther I go, the higher the wall, and I see more of my people's syllables.

Excited as I am, I'm too hungry to look farther. I roll up the poncho and hide it and the knapsack in a gap behind the wall and go in search of breakfast.

I find a patch of Solomon's seal, find a digging stick, and scrabble at them until I dig up the roots. I eat them raw and unwashed, crunching dirt. Then I follow the stream lower and find the elderberry bushes I'd seen as I came up the night before. It was getting dark and I was too tired to pick them. I eat some and then wet my shoulder and sit beside the stream where there's an overhanging bank. A good place for fish. I sit so quietly all sorts of little creatures come out right beside me, a chickadee, a pica, a marmot. . . . Not everything has gone south or lower down. Not everything is hibernating yet.

      🌙   🌙   🌙

ALLUSH

HE WAKES YELLING. I ALMOST JUMP OUT FROM behind the wall to see what's wrong, but I don't want him to see me until I find out more about him.

And people from the Down have guns. (We do, too, but no bullets anymore.)

After he hides his things, I take them and hide them in a spot of my own, but first I examine them. The jacket is worn out and ugly. They call that corduroy. The sweater is worn out, too. It has different colors. It reminds me of when the old ones dressed as tourists. Our parents wore glasses even though they never needed them, and they always had field glasses and cameras and flowery shirts and bright sweaters like this one. I liked when we dressed like that. I used to have a flowery blouse my parents brought me from the Down. If I ever get back there, I'll get myself another one. You need money down there, though. I wonder if there's any somewhere up here or did the old ones use it all up. That's another way to make us have to stay here.

After I examine his things and hide them in a place of my own, I follow where he went, down towards the stream. He limps and leans on his cane. He *is* lopsided. I wince when he eats seal roots without washing them. After that, he heads straight to the elderberry bushes as if he knew they were there. He stuffs berries into his mouth.

Reaching is evidently painful to him. He doesn't use his left arm much. Probably that's also burned but I can't see under his shirt.

After gobbling berries . . . it's got to be including stems, I've never seen anybody this hungry . . . he stops by the stream, takes off his shirt, wets it and holds it to his face and shoulder. As he sits and soaks himself, he watches the fish that always rest under the ledge. I suppose he's thinking how to catch them. Then he sits so still in the shadows of the blowing leaves, I almost don't see him anymore. I sit still, too, (our second lesson) and watch.

Our first lesson was the freeze. How *not* to ever use it. I never understood why not. I don't think the stare that immobilizes is unknown here. Why is it forbidden? Also I wonder—if it's never practiced— can it still be there at all? I know I have it. I've tried it a few times—on animals that is, but never on people.

☽   ☽   ☽

LORPAS

WHEN I COME BACK TO PICK UP MY BUNDLE, MY few belongings are gone. My matches, my flashlight, my pan, my sweater. . . .

I hid them well. Someone must have seen me. I hate to think what the night will be like without my tarp or without matches. I had been looking forward to cooking the Solomon's seal next time and to roasting a fish. And who took it? I hope one of my own kind.

I follow the wall I slept next to, yet higher, slowly, looking for my bundle, but also at everything else. I use my cane to probe likely spots where my bundle might be. Farther on, the wall is almost as high as my head. I pull away some of the brush and see the faint tracing of an animal. A *lorp*. I remember what it's called in my own language because it's the beast I'm named for. Mother drew it for me often. Side view just like this, its feathery topknot raised, its mouth open in a grin of warning. Though small and usually friendly, it was fierce if need be. It was used to guard entrances, sometimes in the real and sometimes, as here, in effigy. Mother said we were too civilized on our world to need them in the real anymore. Besides, she said, our people only had towers now. All of them looking as if they'd lift into the air at any minute, unlike anything on this world.

If there's a *lorp*, there should be an entrance nearby but I don't see one.

I climb the wall with the aid of a sapling growing next to it. Several steps beyond there's a tall doorway with trees right in front of it. It's of stone. I can't budge it. I knock. Foolishly. I actually knock on rock and scrape my knuckles. I examine it more closely. It's part of the granite cliff it's set in. Why would anyone make a huge phony doorway in the forest directly behind trees so you can hardly see it?

I go on. I find a stone gateway (flanked by *lorps*) and go through it. Just beyond it, on a fallen log I find my pan, and in it there's a small piece of dried meat. Looks like squirrel or gopher—or maybe rat.

I sit beside the pan. I look. I listen. Silence, except the general rustle of the forest. Ground squirrels, juncos, jays.

I say, "Thank you."

I'm glad my voice is husky and low like all my people's.

I chew on the stringy meat.

Then I hear a sound high in the top of the trees. My kind were never known for climbing. We're strong but chunky, heavy people. Awkward at such things. I look up. I can't see much but there's somebody up there.

I say, "Thank you," again, then, "Please come down."

It holds stone still. That's like one of us. But natives can do that, too.

"Please."

But it won't.

I wait a bit more, then take my pan and go on. Listening, watching, looking up.

I find a grand stairway—must be twelve or so, wide but low steps, and behind it, another great doorway with a whole row of *lorps* across the top. Though it looks more real than the other door, I can't move it.

As I turn back I find the jacket lying on the steps.

I sit beside it and look up. As before, there's some-body in the trees.

"Come on down. I won't hurt you."

As I sit, I see what might be a window, low and narrow, and only about five or six inches above-ground. I notice it because the glass catches the light when the leaves blow. Just beyond, there's what might be a chimney. It looks to be made out of a rusty tin can. There's a wisp of smoke rising from it.

I go to examine the window. I lie down and try to look in, but it's too dark. Definitely a window though, made from an odd-shaped chunk of broken glass. Just beyond, I find what might be a doorway. I think, here, at last, may be a door I can enter, but that, too, is fake. I can open it, but it goes into a mass of tree roots. Impossible to pass beyond them.

I hear a noise, look up fast and see someone close above me. Clearly one of my own kind, wild red streaked hair, a dirty face. Doesn't this place have combs or washcloths? She . . . I think a woman . . . ducks out of view.

"Thank you for the meat."

I hear the cracking of branches as she moves, in a hurry, farther away. I say, "Be careful."

Maybe if I talk more.

"My name is Lorpas. I saw the *lorps* in the door-ways."

I know she can see I'm one of us, but I say it any-way. "I'm one of us. From Betasha. A Betasha Bob. Or Boob."

No answer.

"Did you call yourselves Boobys like we did?"

From the sounds, she has come closer. Then I think she's here and I carefully don't turn to look. But then I do, fast, and it's just a ground squirrel.

I get up to explore further. I trust she'll follow.

I come to a great avenue. I pace out its width. Here are the largest trees, as though it had once been tree-lined, but there are so many other big trees growing from the middle of it that only an examining eye could tell, or an imagining mind would guess.

I check another grand staircase on the far side of the Avenue. There's carvings across the riser of every step. At the end of the steps there's a sort of spire. For sure supposed to be at the top of a tower. It doesn't look like much on the ground.

All this is trying to look like what Mother meant by her "white, shining, flying cities," though I don't find anything more remarkable about it than what's on this world. And these buildings are ponderous and more gray than white because of the granite they're carved from. Mother had talked of spires where . . . "flying sails" she called them . . . moored . . . but here, in order to hide, there can't be anything taller than the trees. I suppose it's unfair to compare this town with what it was trying to imitate.

I go on. I push at doors and only manage to open one and that one, huge as it is, opens to a narrow hall. There's a pallet as though someone slept there, in the dark, windowless cupboard.

As I come down the steps, I scare a deer and wonder that it's still up here in the cold. Then I see it limps as I do and then I see it's hobbled. Perhaps part of the larder for later.

I'm doing the right thing by ignoring her. She wants to be noticed. She starts dropping pinecones on me. I sit on the stairway and let myself be pelted.

I talk again.

"How well you climb. I always thought our kind wasn't good at that."

Silence.

"How well you throw. You never miss."

". . . ."

"Down below, with the hoodwinked, my name was Norman North. Do you have a native name?"

". . . ."

"I've lived my life below with all my food store-bought. All my clothes, too."

I say that because hers aren't. What I could see of them looked pieced and patched. And that tough piece of dried meat. . . . I couldn't guess what it was.

"I don't know what it's like to live up here. I wouldn't know how."

She doesn't come down.

I get up to do more exploring. The pelting stops but now and then I hear her above me in the trees. I keep to the avenue. It's hard unless one watches for what might be the curb. I come upon a park. It's surrounded by a low wall that has intaglio portraits of odd plants. The wall is pink tuff. The stones would have had to have been brought from the pink cliff far below. I kneel and study the carved flowers. Mother drew several of these for us but some are new to me. I start naming the ones I know out loud. When I get to *allush*, I hear her drop—a safe distance away. I don't look. This time I know it's not a ground squirrel.

Allush, a tiny flower that grows in clusters and only opens in the light of the blue ice moon when that moon is full. Its fringed leaves have a yellow center and blue outside. It was one of Mother's favorites.

I say, "Allush," again.

I turn around, carefully staring at my feet. I sit on the wall. Then I look.

She's cross-legged on the ground a few yards away.

I haven't seen any of my own kind since my parents died, my sister left, and I went off on my own without an address. I'm fascinated. I'm trembling with. . . . I hardly know what. Anticipation? Joy? Yes, joy. This whole place. The secret city that I've always wished for, always hoped really did exist. And now this woman.

She's dressed in tan leather, lines of green and red stitching all over it, holding it together, but also forming symmetrical designs. It imitates pine needles and helps to hide her in the trees. On her feet are moccasins exactly like the Indians of this land used to wear. Her great mop of black hair is streaked with the red typical of my people when they get in the sun. It's matted and tangled. Have they gone completely wild up here? But how could they not?

I must look as odd to her as she does to me. I need a shave and my mustache needs trimming. My hair has grown out after they shaved my head when I was in jail. (Ruth gave me my latest haircut. Not the best I ever had.) I must look naked to somebody used to a full head of hair and maybe to bearded men.

We stare at each other. I can't help smiling. She must see how happy I am—must see how I'd like to run to her and hug her. I hope I don't look too predatory. Hard as I try, I can't wipe that grin off my face.

Finally I say, "Hello."

She nods. A quick dip of the head.

"Can you speak?"

She nods.

"I'll bet your name is Allush."

Another nod.

"I'll bet you've never seen an *allush* any more than I've seen a *lorp*."

Finally a slight smile.

"Allusha. Allusha." I added the "ah" as if she was my lover. I'm so delighted I couldn't help it. I've never said that to anybody. How can it be on the tip of my tongue?

She flinches. If she wasn't sitting down, she'd have run away.

"I'm sorry."

We sit. Silent. I'm finding it hard to just sit when what I want to do is grab her and hug, but I don't want to scare her.

We're so quiet ground squirrels rustle right next to us. A jay flies down, landing inches from Allush's knee. I'll bet she's tamed them all.

Then, like an apparition, slowly, delicately, as if on tiptoe . . . out from the underbrush comes a white mule. She's like a fairyland creature—as if out of an old tale told by the grandmothers. I almost expect her to have a unicorn horn.

The mule leans down and Allush reaches up, touches. . . . Tips of fingers to pinkish nose.

For a moment it's magic, no sound, no rustlings even, and then the mule throws back her head and gives a great hee-haw, hee-haw, hee-haw.

     🌙   🌙   🌙

ALLUSH

HE LOOKS SO HAPPY AT SEEING ME. I CAN SEE IT

hurts him to smile but he can't stop. No one has ever been this glad to see me ever before.

But then Pashty comes, makes a great noise and then trots away.

We laugh and he gets up and reaches towards me and I get up, too. We stare and reach but don't touch. He's one of us for sure—those aluminum-colored eyes.

Then we sit on the wall side by side, again carefully not touching. I hadn't thought he'd feel as shy as I do but he does.

He wants to talk but hardly dares. He keeps starting to say something and then doesn't. So we just sit.

Then there's the sound of air, a swish. I know that sound. I shout, "No!" almost before it lands. An arrow. It hits him and he falls over backwards off the wall. I'm thinking he's dead. I feel awful. Just when there's a whole new person here, he's gone already.

I jump down beside him.

He's flat on his back. Stunned. But he's not dead. The arrow is stuck in his arm.

There's not much blood now, but there might be if I try to get it out.

At least down here we're protected by the wall.

I know who did it. There's nobody else who would. I wonder if he'll shoot me, too.

I stand up and yell, "Youpas! Stop!"

Another arrow plinks into the wall beside me as though to warn me. Would he really?

And another.

I duck behind the wall again and huddle next to this new one called Lorpas.

We could crawl along the wall until we come to Mollish's hut. She'll know what to do.

"Can you crawl?"

"Wait a minute. Just a minute."

He lies there, and then, slowly, turns over on hands and knees. I lead the way.

At Mollish's, I push aside the brush and open the door. Mollish helps me pull him in, but when I tell her Youpas shot him, she's angry that I would haul in a stranger who's been shot by one of us. She says she won't help, and I say I'll use her things and help him anyway, and she says, "Well, I won't stop you if that's what you have to do." I say, "Youpas always shoots first and then asks who it is."

First thing, I give Lorpas elderberry liqueur and herbs to chew to put him out while Mollish sits at the table looking cross.

I cut away his shirt and reveal, not only the injury, but the burns on his other shoulder. As I examine his wound I see the home-call.

"Look, he has a beacon. His mother really cared about him. She must have given him hers. She wanted him to go home." I say those first words in our language we all learned before we could hardly even call our Mamas. "I'm us of one-eighty-nine. Take me home."

Mollish says, "Home!" as if disgusted with the whole idea.

I pull out the arrow. Suddenly there's a lot of blood.

Mollish makes a disgusted noise again, kneels beside me and takes over. "Don't just sit there, start wiping up the blood. It's my floor."

It's just a packed earth floor. I don't know why she cares about it so much and why right now, but I scrape off the bloody layer and put it on the trash. Maybe she just doesn't want me to watch or get in the way.

When she's almost done she says, "Well, shall I leave the beacon?"

"I don't know if he wants to go home or not."

"You want to."

"Of course I do. Isn't that why we're waiting here?"

She says one of her dirty words. She knows them in lots of languages. There aren't any in our own language. That says something about us being better than the natives. We never needed words like those.

I say, "It's better on our home world. Well isn't it?" But I know she was a servant of some sort when she came over. For her it was different. Except she got to be the most important one up here because of her wisdom and her nursing.

She says, "Some used to say so. They wanted things I didn't care about."

"We'd better not take it out. We'd better wait till we can ask him."

"It's now or now. If he wants it he can keep it in

his pocket. And he'll have to leave here anyway. I have enough to do without looking after him and trying to keep him from getting shot again."

If he goes, I hope it's to the Down and that he'll take me with him.

Mollish hands me the beacon. "Get rid of that right away if he doesn't want it, or better yet give it to me and I'll lock it in the vault with the others."

"I'll get rid of it."

I put it in my inside pocket and button it in. I'm going to keep it. I like having one all to myself instead of depending on the vault. Having one, means I won't have to stay here in the city to get taken home. I won't tell Lorpas and I especially won't tell Mollish.

◐   ◐   ◐

LORPAS

I WAKE TO A GREAT CREAKING AND GROANING. THE whole room is shaking. Bits of earth trickle down the walls. The ceiling is low and slants inwards, corbelled. The walls are earth and stones. Tree roots grow down them. I'm underground. The trees above must be waving in the wind. It must be storming.

There are two narrow dirty windows, high on the walls. A low door is cut into the roots on one side. There's a small stove opposite. Its chimney goes up the wall, across the ceiling, and into the wall above the door. Probably to heat a room beyond.

The ceiling is too low. I wonder if I can stand up. I wonder if I can squeeze out that little door. It's too warm. I start to sweat. I'm breathless. I can't stay here. I get up off the pallet. I'm dizzy, but I have to get out of here.

The door sticks. Or did they lock me in? I kick at it. Both my shoulders hurt, but I can't stand this place one second more. I bounce my whole weight against the door. It breaks. I rush into the next room.

Allush and that other woman are there, cross-legged on the floor. It's a bigger room and has a higher ceiling, but even so I have to get out. I rush at the door in front of me. No, that's a closet or is it a vestibule? I push at the back.

Allush yells, "This way, this way." And shows me another door. I rush up stone steps and out, lift my face into the hail and wind, and can breathe again.

That older woman (one of the old ones, still alive!) stands in the doorway. "What? What's wrong? Is he crazy?"

I collapse down on a boulder. I'm pelted with hail but glad to be out of there.

Allush pulls at me. "Come back. You're not well."

"I can't stay underground."

"Where should I put you? You'll get shot again."

She pulls me under a tumbledown roof not far from the . . . what to call it, the burrow? Sits beside me. The wind is blowing the hail sideways. The old one comes out with a tarp for us to huddle under and then goes back in. She doesn't approve of me. I can see it on her face.

"Are you all against me?"

"*I'm* not."

"How many are here?"

"We haven't counted up. The old ones kept track, but we don't bother anymore. We're less and less all the time. It could just be us now, Mollish, Youpas, and me."

"Are all your houses like that?"

"You'll freeze out here and you have to hide."

I turn and flop down so I'm flat on my back.

"Are you feeling all right?"

I'm not. Not at all. Now that I'm out from underground and not feeling claustrophobic, I realize how weak and dizzy and sick I feel.

"You can't stay here."

"I'd rather."

She pulls the tarp up close around me. Says, "I know a place. I'll go open it. Rest here now, but then you'll have to walk. It's across the avenue."

All the way across the street! I wonder if I'll have to climb stairs. Maybe I could crawl. I wonder where my cane is. Probably back where I got shot. Plenty of wood for a new cane here, but that one belonged to my friend Ruth.

Then I remember my beacon. I feel at my armpit
to see if it's gone and it is. Finally and thank goodness. They must have taken it out along with the
arrow. I hope they took it well away from here.

I listen to hail on the tumbledown roof and the
tarp. This had seemed like a paradise. And I could—
sort of could—see what Mother meant. There's a
kind of grandeur to the phony buildings different
from what the natives have. I want to stay. Maybe
with Allush. If she doesn't mind a disfigured cripple.
But if everybody lives underground, and if one of
my own kind already hates me enough to shoot
me. . . .

I doze. Maybe pass-out. I don't know how long it
takes until they come back. Allush and that woman.

"This is Mollish. She'll help."

She's not dressed all in skins as Allush is. She's
wearing worn out store-bought clothes. A black
turtleneck and torn black jeans, faded so as to be
almost white in spots. Over them she wears what
looks like a rabbitskin vest—several skins all pieced
together.

I thought all the old ones would have died by now,
but Mollish is still going. Pure white hair. Handsome—in our way, the natives wouldn't think so. It
can't be easy for an old person to live up here. The
ground all around the Secret City is rough and
rocky. Even rocky right in the middle of the city. But
I can feel how strong she is as they help me, one on
each side, across the street and up the steps. They

argue about me every slow step of the way. Mollish doesn't want me around. I ask why not?

"We're getting along just fine without you."

The huge, huge door carved out of the granite cliff is open just far enough for us to squeeze in. I don't think it can open any farther. Inside there's a cavernous hall. Four small windows near the ceiling. More just holes than windows. An oil lamp burns in the middle of the floor, even so it's dark. Dust flies about. They've brought a pan of broth and a little stove. It's cold. Much colder than outside. I suppose Allush thought this room would be big enough to be all right for me but it isn't.

Again ... all of a sudden I have the energy. I squeeze out the door and sit down on the steps— again breathless. I can't imagine anybody, neither us nor the natives, being able to live like that. And I'm not more claustrophobic than most. Or at least not that I knew until this.

Now that I'm out of there I'm cold. The hail has stopped but the wind is still blowing. Trees are still whipping back and forth. Allush and the other one come and stand in the doorway again.

"What will we do with him?"

The old one says, "Take him to where the archeologists camped."

Allush says, "He'll never make it that far. Besides, Youpas will shoot at us again."

"I'll be with you. He won't shoot when I'm there."

We get started. But I only have energy when I'm scared of being closed in. Even with one of them on each side I can't go far. When I get to the bottom of the long stairway I sit down to rest.

And then, again, silent, mysterious, magic, and at the perfect time . . . comes the white mule. They help me up on her slippery back, I hold her scant mane and she tiptoes me down to a lean-to at the edge of town.

They set me up with the tarp hanging down across the front and leave to go back to get the lamp and the food. I hear the mule moving around outside. Having her there cheers me. I wish they'd left the tarp open so I could watch her. I curl and collapse into my pain. They'll bring me something for that. It won't be long.

But then the tarp swings open and there's a man, a quiver of arrows and an unstrung bow slung across his shoulders. He's dressed like some sort of Daniel Boone. A mountain man. A scraggly beard, another mop of hair. They *have* gone wild.

I sit up. I wonder if I still have my knife or did Allush or maybe that woman take it? I don't dare check my pockets. He hasn't said anything, but I keep my hands in view.

If he wanted to kill me before, he'll no doubt want to now. I'm in no shape to fight. And he's one of us, so just as strong as I am.

He says something in our old language, but I've forgotten it.

"I can't speak Betasha anymore."

But he goes on in our language.

I shake my head. "I don't understand."

I start to get up. I don't want him attacking me while I'm sitting down.

He kicks me. I should have grabbed his foot and pulled him over, but he kicked my wounded shoulder. I gasp and fall back. I say, "I'm one of you," though he's knows that. Maybe that's why he hates me.

I turn on all fours and try to get up, but he kicks me again and I'm flat on my back.

Last time I used the freeze it didn't work on my own kind, they just laughed, but I can't think of anything else to do.

I stare into his eyes. I hold stone still. Eyes. . . . That's all I see. All I know. It's as if I'm looking through a dark tunnel with his eyes at the end of it.

First I see surprise there, and then nothing . . . a blank. He tries to turn away. It takes a moment but then he's stone still, too. Two stones facing each other. I, breaking the rule of lesson number one not to ever do this on this world. Except this is my own kind.

I mustn't let go. How long will it take? How long *can* it take?

FINALLY ALLUSH AND THAT OLD ONE COME. I LET GO and he falls back with an angry shout and more of our language. And then they're all jabbering away in our language. I'm exhausted and he looks to be, not only angry, but as drained as I am. He's shaking. Could be with rage. If he wanted to kill me before, he wants to even more now.

I interrupt. In English. I say I'll leave as soon as I can. Just let me rest a couple of days and I'll get out of here.

They talk more in our language. I recognize a word or two here and there but useless ones like "and" and "maybe" and "tomorrow." I notice, too, that Allush and the man sprinkle their talk with a lot of native words as if they weren't that good in their own language either.

Finally the old one says, "All right. Long as you're gone within a week."

I didn't think they'd give me even that much time.

Then the old one says, "The freeze. . . . That was unfair. Haven't you been trained not use it?"

"There wasn't anything else to do—that I could see. He wants to kill me."

Then she talks to the man, again in our lan-guage. Scolding him. (I remember, but, and, therefore, and the little fill in words all languages have: "for," "uh," "like," "you know" . . . things like that.)

Finally he leaves. The old one and Allush set out the things they've brought. The little smoky pot of fire and the broth, blankets, a sleeping pad.

I feel as if I've never been this tired in my life. I fall asleep before the soup is heated.

I WAKE TO SHOUTS . . . WAILS, ACTUALLY . . . OF horror. I jump up, almost trip over the fire pot and the soup heating there and rush out. Allush and the old one are outside and before them is a limp pile of red and white. My God, it's the mule. The beautiful white mule with her throat cut.

Allush and the old one kneel beside her. They're stunned.

Nothing to be done. Nothing to say. I kneel beside them.

We all know who did it.

I feel for my knife. They did leave it.

Without me here it wouldn't have happened.

"I'm so sorry. I'm sorry I came. Without me. . . ."

Allush says, "It's not your fault."

"It is."

If I wasn't so burned and then shot, I'd go after him right now. But I have to wait. And this isn't my city. I don't know my way around.

Allush says, "This isn't the first thing he's done like this, but it's the worst. I never thought he'd go this far."

But she can't talk anymore. Then she manages to say, "I'm not staying here. Ever. I'm going with Lorpas."

She doesn't know me anymore than I know her. She may be sorry she said it and I may be sorry, too. I don't even trust my own: "Love at first sight." That's what it was. Besides, it's not me she wants to go with, she just wants to get away. But I feel happy even so. When has there ever been someone among my own kind who's a suitable mate for me? And it's easy to see she likes me.

We all feel too bad to eat, but they insist I have the broth. Even the old one who obviously can't wait to be rid of me. She's one of those people that'll help either side of any war or any kind of hurt creature. When she sees how I'm in pain even trying to eat, she feeds me. She uses a battered stainless steel spoon. Everything's old and scratched, the pan and the fire pot, too.

The dead mule lies right outside. They can't drag it away. I could help if I had even one good arm. The body will attract wolves and maybe even a mountain lion. Best not to be near it. They'll move me instead. They want to hide me in a different spot anyway in case that man comes back.

This time we won't have the mule to help me move. And this time I'm worse off than ever. After eating, all I want to do is lie where I am. And I don't think they know where to take me. Just away.

I lean on them. I stumble. Each time I fall and don't want to get up, they say, "Just a few more yards," but I don't think they know where they're going.

Where they finally put me isn't a shelter at all. Just under a tree where the branches hang down around us. We have to push through them to get to the sheltered spot next to the trunk. Then they go back and get the pan and blankets.

They're going to spend the night with me. I'm already asleep when I feel them tucking me in. The old one doesn't like me but even so, what sweet, sweet women—both of them.

◐   ◐   ◐

ALLUSH

I couldn't talk before but now I can't stop talking. Mollish listens. At least Lorpas is sleeping through it.

"What an evil thing! How could anybody? We loved her. We need her. How can she be dead? I know exactly what happened. She would have come right up to him. She would have put her head on his chest. She'd have come to be killed. And then, just as if one of our deer for the larder. . . . Has anything ever happened here as bad as this? We're as bad as the natives. When one of the old ones died I was sad but it was a normal thing. It was holding hands. People sang. How could this have happened?"

And then I say it all over again.

Mollish doesn't say anything. She holds me. I cry. I miss the cosy burrow, but I feel safe in her arms.

Except where is there any safety if Pashty can die like this? And from one of us? Us!

If Lorpas hadn't come. . . . Youpas always thought I belonged to him but I never ever did nor wanted to.

At least Youpas would never think we'd hide under a tree. We're below the city and away from the trail. I hope he's back there checking to see if we're in any of the burrows. That'll keep him busy all night.

IN THE MORNING, fIRST LIGHT, WE MOVE LORPAS yet farther down—beyond the elderberries. We stay away from the stream-side path so it's hard going. He probably misses his cane. I'd go back and get it, but I'm scared to. I'd rather make him a new one.

We always let Youpas do all the butchering. He must have gotten used to blood. Cutting throats is a normal thing to him.

We don't talk at all. We feel too bad. Lorpas limps his usual limp. He's using a dead stick for a cane. We try to help him but it's hard with so much brush in the way.

And here's a hut I never knew about before. Hidden behind rocks and trees. It's not one of ours. Looks like an old miner's hut. How did Mollish know about it? Though the old ones must have examined this whole valley before they built the city.

It's made of logs caulked with moss. Must be a hundred years old yet still solid. Door at one end and window at the other. No glass, but shutters. It's dirty and dusty and full of cobwebs. We spread our blankets and lie down anyway. I was awake all night last night, but this time I fall asleep right away.

I don't know what we'll do when Mollish dies. I should have paid attention more. I shouldn't have spent all my days climbing trees and making pets of everything.

When I wake Mollish is gone. The sun slants sideways in through the doorway. It looks to be late afternoon. How could I have slept so long, uncomfortable on the floor with no pallet? You'd think I was the wounded one. Lorpas is outside in the sun, sitting with his back against the doorway. I'm relieved to see him. I was worried he might have left us all on his own to protect us from himself.

I go and sit beside him. Maybe now I'll have a chance to talk to him. I'm not as afraid of him as I was. I want to talk about going back to the Down.

LORPAS

SHE COMES OUT AND SITS ON THE OTHER SIDE OF the doorway. Not too close. We look at each other but then, shy, we look out at the view. We're about as low in the valley as you can get. Everything is up from here. I can see part of the rocky path where I first scrambled and stumbled and fell, down into this valley. A little river isn't far. You can't see it, but you can hear it bubbling. The miner or shepherd or hunter who built this hut had a good spot. I've seen this kind of hut in these mountains before. Twice I spent nights in ones just like it on the way here. They're not built for anything but sleep and shelter in a storm. The ceiling is so low a man my size has to hunch over but it's light and airy. Not like being in a burrow. There's never a chair or table. The fireplace for this one is outside a couple of yards beyond me. It has a log next to it for a bench.

I have questions I want to ask, but I see her screwing up her courage to talk so I keep silent. Just when I think she isn't going to speak, she says, "Are there more white mules down there?"

I think how delicate and beautiful that one was. How she looked as if she belong in the forest. I say, "Never another exactly like that."

"How could he do that? How could anybody?"

There's never anything to answer with things like this. I just shake my head.

She says, "We're no different from the natives," and I say, "I never thought we were."

"I thought that's why the old ones wanted us to stay away from them. So we wouldn't get to be evil and nasty and believe ignorant things."

"We're no better. Look what our people did to me. These burns are from our own kind. They wouldn't even talk to me. I was yelling, No, but they tried to snatch me home, anyway."

She looks horrified. "But the old ones said Betasha was. . . ."

"I don't want to go home. They burned me when I tried to fight them off. I never believed the old ones when they said our world was better or that we were better. Our kind even burned the old lady I lived with. Killed her for no reason. They were laughing. They thought nothing of it. She was a native but she was like a mother to me."

I see I've started her thinking. She says, "That's what Mollish thinks. She doesn't want to go home either but all the other old ones hated it here."

"So did my parents. My poor mother couldn't stop talking about how beautiful the homeworld was."

We're looking out at a gnarled juniper, the blue sky behind it dotted with little balls-of-cotton clouds that look phony, next to us are rocks with orange lichen. A black and yellow striped lizard runs past the rocks. The stream gurgles.

"Look how beautiful it is right here."

"Well. . . ."

"Don't you think so?"

I guess she doesn't. She says, "How do you know it's not better back home? They all said so."

"Mother exaggerated. I don't think having two moons can be that much better than one. Golden grass on rolling hills. . . . We have that here. And sometimes poppies as far as the eye can see. Have you seen that?"

She hasn't.

"I'll show you. It has to be in the spring though. Will you come with me?"

Now she looks shy again. And pleased. She looks away and then a quick glance at my face as though wondering if I'm serious.

"I mean it. Come with me."

I can see in her eyes she'd go anywhere with me.

I take her hand. She doesn't pull away.

We sit.

But then, suddenly, silently, here's Mollish. She's sitting in front of us before we know she's there. She has so much to carry. I don't know how she did it by herself. Two backpacks, and a package.

Allush jumps up. Says, "We're leaving. Are we? I hate it here. I can't wait to get back to the Down."

How can she hate it? The way she swings around in the trees? The way she knows her way around the Secret City and as silently as Mollish? I would have thought she'd hate being in so-called civilization. She must have forgotten what it's like. Life up here would suit me—if I built myself a good cabin.

Or maybe she wants to leave because of the mule. I can understand that.

But if we are going back, I have to tell them I escaped from jail.

"I can't go out the way I came in. The natives may

even think I'm the one that burned my friend. Our own people did it but they'll think I did. They don't know anything about us Betashas. Besides, I escaped from jail."

Mollish says there's only one way out. And I'd better leave here before I get shot again. Anybody who'd kill the mule has gone crazy. Besides, she, also, has wanted to come back to the Down. This life is fine in the summer, but she's too old for another winter up here. She says she'll come back in the spring.

I say, "I'll come back with you," and Allush says, "Please don't."

Mollish says we should start now and be careful. Youpas may follow. She says, "These will help," and hands me leaves. "For pain. For energy. Chew them."

It's clear right away that her way out is not the same way I came slipping and sliding in. It's easier. We don't have to climb that cliff I scrambled down. For sure we won't end up in the same little town where I was in jail, we're heading too far south for that.

I wonder if the cops would recognize me anyway with a half-grown beard and longer hair and I've lost a lot of weight. I hate to look too scruffy in among the natives. I do have two of Ruth's pink razors left. I'll save them for later.

Again, the straps of my backpack rub my shoulders. I've healed a lot, mostly from the herbs Mollish covered them with, but with this rubbing they'll get worse again. At least the day is half over, we'll have to stop soon.

Her way out, though easier, is just as spectacular as my way in—rows of snowy peaks, glaciers. . . . When thirsty we chew on frazzle ice. There are narrow paths on ledges that are straight down thousands of feet on one side and one place that's straight down on both sides. That one scared me. I guess Allush is used to heights from being in the trees, and Mollish, though she's wobbly, does well, too. If they can do it, so can I.

The first night we don't dare build a fire. We sit in a circle as though around a campfire and eat the dried meat Mollish brought. At first we don't talk much, but then Allush says, "Tell me about the Down. It must have changed. We left when I was eight. That was eighteen, maybe nineteen years ago."

I thought she was younger. I suppose, alone out here, she didn't have a chance to grow up.

"It's not changed that much."

But then she tells me more about the Up than I tell her about the Down.

"In the summer campers sometimes come almost to the city. We used to dress as campers and roam about being friendly to everybody. We'd steal things. But we don't have anymore camping clothes."

And we talk about mules. Allush says, "Mules helped us get up to the city. Of course by now those are all dead. Pashty was brought up not so long ago. We've always felt close to mules. We like to think we're like them: for their surefooted hardiness, and for the three Fs just like ours: Fight, Flight, or Freeze. Their freeze is because they're smart enough to stand still . . . to refuse to do anything dangerous."

We spread our sleeping bags in a row. I go to sleep holding Allush's hand.

WE HAVE FOOD WITH US, BUT ALSO I'M GOOD AT snatching fish bare-handed as long as there's a still pool somewhere in the streams. Mollish and Allush are impressed. I think Mollish is beginning to like me in spite of herself. She arranges my backpack straps in a way that saves my burns some. Allush smiles whenever she looks at me. This whole trip is wonderful . . . because of being with her. Actually being with both of them.

The next night we feel it's safe to build a fire. I cook the fish. We arrange our sleeping bags near the fire, I on the far side as if as a guard. And I do consider myself a guard. Nothing I'd rather do than guard these two women.

THREE DAYS OUT AND WE'RE ON ONE OF THOSE rocky paths, single file, a steep drop on our left and straight up on our right. The trail is, at most, two or three feet wide . . .

. . . when here are our rescuers, come to snatch us all home.

Again, I'm ashamed of them—soft, doughy, pale, their hair in fancy pompadours, dressed as if for Hawaii, even to shorts. Easy to see they're ignorant of this world. They stand as if surprised to find themselves on a ledge, the view of mountains beyond. They're single file as we are. I'm last. Allush is in front. Everybody's standing still. Stunned. Both they and us.

I say, "I thought none of us had a beacon."

Allush says, "I have yours."

Mollish says, "But I told you. . . ."

Allush, ahead of us, says, in our language . . . that first phrase all our mother's taught us, even before we could hardly say anything at all. I still know it by heart. "I'm us. Take me home."

And before she can say anymore, she's gone. Off in a pinkish haze. A sort of ectoplasm . . . that's all that's left of her. For a moment it stays in her shape, then she . . . it . . . blows away.

Perhaps she thought I'd be right behind her. But Mollish and I both shout, "No!"

It's almost the same as it was back when they tried to snatch me before, though the men seem more wary than they were then and they're obviously frightened to find themselves on the edge of a drop off.

Mollish pushes the tube aimed at her down and to the side, so the man in front of her burns the ground instead of us. She's strong and she can kickbox, but there's only a narrow place to fight. She's off balance. She kicks a good kick, then off she goes, with the man she kicked right behind her, both sliding down the scree in a dusty landslide.

I don't know what happens to the third man. I'm too busy fighting the one that's after me. I'm wounded and burned, but I'm in better shape than he is. I swing my cane—the one Allush made for me—hard. It breaks but it knocks him off balance. Then I come in close and knock him out with one good uppercut. Why don't they ever send people who can defend themselves even a little bit? And they know nothing about the natives nor of us who grew up here. Some of the tourists must have gotten back before they stopped picking us up. Some of those tourists must have told them about this world. And why don't they sit down and talk with us even for just a minute? Give us a chance to think about it and choose if we want to go home or not and if we do, give us a chance to say good-bye? They think we don't know enough to decide for ourselves. Mollish knows both worlds and wants to stay.

I have to get down to her to see if she's all right.

Except I don't want this man trying to send me home again when my back is turned. But that was a good punch. He's out cold. I examine his instruments, strange small tubes with little paper clip

things as switches. I wouldn't dare flip any of them.
I'd like to get rid of them and him—send him home
though I don't know how. I wonder if Mollish
remembers how to use these.

I look under his arms and as far as I can see there's
no beacon. Yet they can't want to be stuck here any
more than our parents did.

I take his tubes, then I go along the trail until
there's a way to climb down. I toss his tubes down in
front of me, take off my backpack. Then I leave the
trail and start down. I hope Mollish is all right. It's a
long fall but she's tough. For sure tougher than they
are.

Allush wanted to go home. I shouldn't feel bad
though I do. Did she really want to go back without
me? Or did she think I'd follow? She's the only
woman of my own people. . . . And she liked me.

●   ●   ●

ALLUSH

I CAN'T TAKE IT IN. SPIRES, DAZZLE, CHIRPING AND
cheeping. A distant humming. The air has a kind of
glitter. Could that be? Maybe it's all inside my head.
But it's wonderful even so. I knew I was right to

come back. The Secret City was supposed to be like the cities of home, but it wasn't. It was supposed to remind our parents and show us younger ones what the home planet was like, but how could it? Everything had to hide under the trees and here it's all towers and shine! They couldn't have had any of this. And, with everything made of granite, there was nothing but gray. Here I can't tell what I'm seeing. I hardly know where one tower begins and another ends.

Porches. Are those really porches? Tethered? Like square boats but in the air? Our parents should have told us. But maybe they tried and we didn't understand.

And those doorways! I'm sure they really open and not just into a closet or into nothing.

Those sounds might be birds. Our parents said there were lots of birds . . . that almost everything was birds. There's something twirling in the distance. Do their birds twirl instead of fly?

There's this silvery haze. It looks as if it's raining though it isn't. Little white puffy things like seeds are falling out of the sky. Everything that should be green is reddish. There's a bitter smell. I'm not sure if I like it or not. But this is home! This is what I've waited for all my life. How can I not like it?

I think to move closer to get a better look at the buildings, and then I realize I'm on a platform above everybody else—as if on display and there's a dead man lying right beside me. He's wearing a ridiculous outfit. It's those clothes they all thought the natives wore but they hardly ever did—except in Hawaii. But everybody here is colorful. I'm the one, looks drab. I'm in my worn deerskin outfit. And I'm dirty. They all have fancy hairdos, black hair even curling round their eyes. Or maybe that's some kind of glasses. I hate to think what *my* hair looks like. I hardly ever comb it anymore. That's because I can't. I did try because of Lorpas being there, but it was in a permanent tangle. I knew I'd have to cut out the knots first. I was going to ask Mollish to help.

Everybody's looking at me. This is a wide central square and they're on wide steps below. They're laughing and trying to hide it. For sure they've never seen somebody from the Secret City until now. To them I'm a barbarian. Well, I am. My parents thought so, too. Mollish thought so, but she didn't care. Why isn't she here? And Lorpas? I thought they were right behind me.

Do these people, trying to hide their smiles, even know there's a dead person lying here? They bow and nod. They wave their hands back and forth in front of their faces as if waving off flies. I don't know if there are flies here but I think that gesture is about me. I wonder if I smell bad. I know I'm dusty and . . . well, I haven't had a good wash-up since it got cold.

The way they're dressed and the way their hair is, I can't tell which are male and which female. But I suppose they can't tell about me either.

I take a step forward but a couple of people grab me from behind, turn me around and rush me away, down steep steps and in a doorway. Out of sight fast as if I'm too horrible to be seen by decent people—as if I might do something dangerous or unseemly.

They put me in a tiny room, a kind of padded cell. There's not even a window and everything in there is gray. I wish there was a window. What's the sense of being here on a whole new world and not seeing anything? I was wanting so badly to see all that glitter and I especially wanted to get a better look at the twirling birds . . . if those are birds. This room might as well be on any old world.

They make me take a whole batch of pills. I try not to, but they know how to force you. I yell both, "No," and, that "Aay *yaa*" of my own language. I call out for Lorpas. Why isn't he here?

But those pills. . . .

. . . AND HERE I AM, COMING-TO.

I'm alone. They've cleaned me up, cut my hair short and put something on it to make it stiff. They've taken away my clothes. I wonder if they destroyed them. I made those myself and decorated them with red and green thread which was hard to get up there at the city.

They've dressed me in a kind of smock, greenish, sprinkled randomly with a few red dots of different sizes. There's writing on the front. I recognize it as writing because it's the same kind that was carved on the walls of the Secret City. I never got that good at reading it. I've no idea what it says. Maybe Watch Out For This Wild Barbarian or maybe Smelly Foreigner, Don't Breathe.

There's no mirror. I've no idea what I look like with my hair all cut off. How will Lorpas know who I am?

There's a little table that wasn't here before. On it, a cup of faintly reddish liquid, and beside that, a dish of what must be something to eat, also reddish and with little black specks in it. I sit on the low stool and sip at the red stuff. It tastes so odd I wonder if they're trying to knock me out again, but I'm so thirsty I drink it anyway. People used to get sick just going from one country to another. What about going from one world to another? I do feel a little queasy. I wonder about all those pills.

I take about half a bite of the food. It tastes so bad I start to laugh, and then I find tears are rolling down my cheeks. I've never been a person who cries much but I cry now. It starts off with the horrible taste and then I think how things would be if Lorpas had come with me. We'd both be laughing at this odd food. I wouldn't feel so lonely and scared if he were here. I know he didn't want to leave there, but I thought he'd go wherever I went. If he'd had time to think, he would have come. I suppose he didn't have time to do anything but act. And then he already got burned once before trying to stay there. I wonder if he's all right this time. Maybe he's burned again and needs help. Of course Mollish is there. Or is she burned, too?

Maybe we'd have come together if we'd been holding hands when they snatched me. We did hold hands now and then. That's as far as we went. We never even kissed. But there wasn't room on the ledge for holding hands.

I wish we hadn't been so shy. You'd think, at our age, we wouldn't have been. He said I was the first of our kind he'd seen in years. He said when he first saw me he couldn't believe I existed, especially since I'd jumped down from the trees right in front of him. He said, "What better way to meet somebody?" That was when we lay close to each other, wrapped tight in our sleeping bags. I was watching his profile with the stars behind it. Even then I wanted to kiss him but I didn't dare. There were times I could see in his eyes that he wanted to kiss me, too. Youpas used to look at me with a kind of glare, accusing me of not loving him. Youpas would have kissed. In fact he tried every now and then, but I wouldn't let him. Lorpas was the opposite. He always looked at me with a shy glance full of a sort of slow kindness. As if there was all the time in the world to enjoy getting to know each other. But there wasn't.

I used to wish that our Neanderthalish faces were like the natives. I wanted a small sharp nose and thinner eyebrows. I wanted fuller, more shapely lips. I wanted to be willowy. I especially wanted a less lumpy forehead, but when I first looked at Lorpas, lying there sleeping at the edge of the Secret City, right away I changed my mind.

I should feel good here where everybody looks like us. I mean their faces. Nothing else about them does, what with those crazy clothes, though I haven't seen much. I wonder if I'll miss the natives' faces, though once we got up to the Secret City I hardly saw them anymore except in picture books. In the beginning we had old movies too, but they got worn out. For a while we could run the projectors, and we could recharge batteries by hand or foot pumps, but that all gave out.

FINALLY THE TWO MEN COME FOR ME. (I KEEP thinking men, but I'm not sure. The clothes don't give me any signals I know of and everybody looks so soft and chubby.) I guess I'm presentable. By now it's darker out. Of course there's the glow of the dust. I know from my parents that it never gets really dark. Maybe I'm not as presentable as I think, since they waited till this twilight time to take me out.

We get onto one of those wobbly porches hanging from nothing, and swing off slowly. In a way I'm scared and in a way I'm not because everything is so fascinating. Besides, would they really put me in danger after they took all the trouble to get me back? I hardly pay attention to my fear except to hang on tight. I stare at the buildings. They're all exactly the same. When I look out over them from the high point of the porch's swing, it makes me think of a field of huge shiny blades of grass. As we start down I stare at the ground where a few people stroll. Not a single one walks fast. There are no streetlights. They're not needed. Nothing is lit except inside the windows. The dust rings and the moons—both at the half-moon stage—are enough so that no lights are needed.

The blue one looks to be a lot farther away than the red. Or is it just smaller? And does one always follow the other like it seems to now?

We touch down a few minutes later.

So far the men haven't talked to me—just to themselves. I think the language has changed some since our parents left fifty years ago, but I understand a lot of it. They're not talking about me but about the colors of something—colors of music, I think they said.

For sure these are males, their voices are gravely. I wonder if they're the ones undressed me and dressed me when I was drugged.

They take me to one of those slim towers. They say, "This is where you'll. . . ." Something or other. Seemed like "collide" or "fall down." Maybe, "crash."

The room is on the twelfth floor. I think twelfth. I'm not sure of our numbers. The elevator comes up the middle so that when we get out there are windows on all sides. I know they have elevators back there, too, but last time I was in one I was eight years old so it's as scary as the porch. All the rooms must be pretty small in these towers, and the higher, the smaller. I'm glad they didn't put me any higher. I wanted to ask them: Is this all just for looks so the towers will all be alike or what? But I didn't.

One says, "Go on loosen up. We'll take you to a. . . ." And another word I don't know. "You'll meet a Special." I think that's what he said.

Then they leave. I wouldn't know how to escape if I wanted to, or even how to go down and take a walk. And I want to . . . at least I want to take a walk. I want to be on my own, wandering the city, but I'd be lost in five minutes.

Everything that happens makes me wish for Lorpas. With him, I'd laugh. Or maybe we'd discover how to go take a walk.

Except it *is* beautiful. From here I can look at all these other spires—as far as you can see, nothing but spires. And the moons. My parents talked of them every time there was a starry night back there, as if two moons was always better than the stars. I try to see those twirling bird things but I guess they're only out in the daytime.

I haven't been to any kind of town since I was a child. The Secret City isn't really a city. We were living like cavemen. Or rather like moles in our burrows.

I'm thirsty and I don't know how to get a drink. I don't even know where they pee. There are buttons for everything but I don't dare push them because the one I did push turned on bright lights, but then wouldn't turn them back off.

I dare to pee into a depression in the floor. I hope that's not where breakfast will appear.

I lie down on the bed. This one is different from the cot in that gray cell. You sink in more than you want to. At first I jump up because I think the bed is going to swallow me, but there's no place else except the floor. And would they really try to eat me? I lie down again. There are no blankets so nothing to hide under to block out the light. The bed seems warm, but I still don't like how it curls up around you. Lorpas would hate it even more than I do, what with his claustrophobia.

To think it was just last night I slept next to him, his hand on my arm. There was the sound of the stream and crickets. Why didn't we kiss then, when we had the chance?

But everything is making me so tired I don't find it hard to sleep . . . that is, after a time of letting tears drip down. At least the bed has no fancy scary way of drying them. But then my hair is a bother. It's stiff and uncomfortable. I don't know what to do about it. Maybe you're supposed to wash it out every night but I can't even get myself a drink. But I do fall asleep soon and sleep soundly.

LORPAS

THE BOTTOM OF THE SCREE IS FULL OF BOULDERS. I find the man first. He's dead. That's a bad sign for Mollish. I'm hoping. . . . I need her. . . . She was such a wonderfully tough and wise lady. She's the only old one I've seen for a long time and she was so unlike all the others in loving this world more than her own. Allush said she'd been a servant and that was why she liked it better here. Makes me wonder about my world. There were things our parents wouldn't talk about. Mother thought she was a cut above even our own people. I'd try to argue with her but she always said there was nothing to say about it, why should she argue? She just was, and if I couldn't see it, it didn't matter to her. She said it wasn't the sort of thing nice people talked about.

At first I can't find Mollish. That's because she's farther up on the steep slide of scree and partly covered up with gravel. When I see her, I think she might be all right—she didn't have that far to fall. I have a hard time getting up to her. I slide down almost as much as I crawl up.

But she's dead. Not a mark on her that I can see. Maybe she was just too old for a fall and a fight.

I dig in my heels and prop myself beside her. It's hard to sit there without sliding.

I sit a long time. I hold her hand. I think how we both liked it here. How she was an old one who could see through all the jingoistic bullshit of our parents. All the more reason, then, that I'm right in wanting to stay. Why didn't I talk to her more? My God, the things I could have found out that my parents never would have told me, but all I did was pay attention to Allush.

I miss her, Allush, Allusha, but I keep telling myself, she got what she wanted. At least that. I hope she's happy there. I hope she can come back if she doesn't like it.

I've no idea how long I sit there—it seems I'm mostly not thinking at all, I just sit—empty—then I see the sun is getting low. If I don't hurry back to the trail, I'll have to sit here all night. I can't climb up in the dark and I left my flashlight back in my pack. And I completely forgot about that man I knocked out. I wonder what mischief he's gotten himself into.

When I take Mollish's backpack and bedroll, she slides the rest of the way down the scree slope. As do I. Her backpack was what was holding her up. I leave her there next to the man. I walk beyond the scree and climb back to my backpack. I sling both packs . . . one on each sore shoulder . . . and go back to check on the man. I may be sorry, but if he's stuck here he won't know what to do. He'll need me.

HE'S SITTING WITH HIS BACK AGAINST THE HIGH side of the trail shivering. He's dressed unsuitably for the side of a mountain in high altitudes and in this season. I unroll Mollish's bedroll and lay it over his shoulders.

I remember that odd jerk of the head, as if to throw back long hair. It means thanks. Mollish did that, too. All the old ones did.

He says something. Though that was my first language, I don't understand. I shake my head, no, but all my gestures are from here, he won't know what that means.

I sit beside him and get out some of our dried food and a canteen of Mollish's tea. He tastes the meat and gags as I would do after half a bite of caterpillar. But he drinks the tea as if he doesn't dare but is too thirsty not to. I don't blame him his fear.

Odd though, that they never bothered to learn one of these languages just in case of getting stuck here. Even when our parents first came they never thought it was important to know more than a few words of English or Spanish. Of course these men have no role but to snatch people back.

I'd climb down and get the tubes I threw over and give them back to him if thought it would help him go home, but I'm afraid he'll snatch me back with him or burn me if I won't come. They all seem to think we'd be better off home whether we want to go or not. I suppose because it's so much more civilized there, but I would have been happy up in the Secret City where it's even less civilized . . . as long as

I didn't have to live underground. I was all set to stay up there. Maybe I would have except for Youpas.

But strange how it was so empty—that I only saw those three people in all my wandering around. I wonder if there are any more of us up there, or if they dwindled away and died or maybe got bored like Allush was and left for the Down or got lost trying to find it. No wonder Youpas was upset that Allush was so taken with me, she's his only hope for a mate, too. For sure, when he finds out we're not there, he'll follow us down, but he doesn't know Allush has gone back to the homeworld. He'll blame me for that.

WE'LL HAVE TO SPEND THE NIGHT ON THE LEDGE. It's going to be a dark, cloudy night. Too dangerous for two of us to walk this rocky trail single-file with just my tiny flashlight.

He's cold even after I wrap him in Mollish's bedroll. And he's frightened. When he looks at me, it's wide-eyed—like a scared baby animal looking at the mother for help. I thought maybe it would be dangerous sleeping with him next to me after I'd knocked him out, but I can see on his face that I'm his only hope.

I make him put on my long underwear over his shorts. I zip him into Mollish's sleeping bag, I squeeze his shoulder. I say, "Sleep now." As I say it,

I use two fingers and shut his eyes for him. "Sleep. Sleep." (He might as well start learning the language.) Of course his eyes pop open again right away.

I lie down. We're head to head, both of us in the only place we can be, stretched out right in the middle of the trail. I turn out the flashlight. No stars, no moon. I wonder what he thinks of night on this world. Jet black. Scary. Maybe tomorrow night he'll get to see stars. I hope so. With their two moons always in the way, my kind can't ever have seen a sky full of stars.

If he comes down with me in the morning, I'll have to do something about that pompadour and that crazy shirt. Shorts for heaven's sake!

I HAVE A HARD TIME SLEEPING. I MISS ALLUSHA. We always slept next to each other, looking up at the stars and the moon—whispering after Mollish had gone to sleep. Mollish knew the stars as much as Ruth did. Sometimes she pointed out the constellations, too. Now both she and Ruth are dead and all my fault.

And there's a big problem, I don't know the way. Neither towards town nor back to the city. If towards town, all I know is east and (I hope) south enough to avoid the town where I was in jail. But going east should be enough. We'll hit Route 395 somewhere. No way to miss it. It goes north and south between two mountain ranges for hundreds of miles.

And Youpas will be following us, waiting for a chance to kill me. When he finds out Allush got snatched and I didn't stop her he'll be after me more than ever. Should I turn back even so? Take this man to the Secret City to hide out there with the beacons and wait for rescue? Try to find it again, that is. But I don't want to have a showdown with Youpas. I'll take him to the Down. Give him a chance to learn a few things about this world. Maybe he can go back and tell our people to stop snatching us without asking. I wonder if it would do any good. Maybe there's a reason they want us back. Could be as simple as that we're dangerous to our own people here. What if we're found out by the natives? Who knows what will happen then. Homo sapiens sapiens off, yet again, to wipe out Neanderthals.

IN THE MORNING WE WAKE TO HAIL AND THUNDER. This ledge is a bad place to be in lightning. Here, there's no shelter whatsoever. I have a decent hat, but he doesn't even have one of those baseball caps the old ones always wore. I put my hat on his head. He says, "Ayyaa, ayyaa," but I say, "Yes." Then he ducks his head as, thanks.

I pack up, give him Mollish's backpack and we hurry on—down and east. I'm not thinking which way to go. I just want to get us back into the tree line to someplace more sheltered. *Then* I'll think. Also, on this rough ground, I need a cane but there won't be any possible sticks until we get into the trees. Thinking cane makes me think of Ruth again. Hers must still be up behind the pink wall where I got shot.

Rain or no, the man stops every now and then and looks around. His stopping makes me stop and look, too. I try to imagine what he's thinking— maybe that everything is ugly compared to his world, just like Mother said it was. Even so, whatever he's thinking, I appreciate the view even more than I normally do. I think: *my* snowy peaks, *my* silvery waterfalls on the mountain across from us, *my*, *my*, *my* beautiful world.

While we're still fairly high, the rain stops. Shortly after it does we watch a turkey vulture soar out from the cliff, just above us. Later, in the trees below, we walk through fireweed as high as our heads. In this sheltered side of the mountain, it's still in bloom. A magpie flies across our path and I hear the man gasp. I guess no magpies back on our home world. I'd rather not be where there aren't any magpies.

We don't stop to eat until we're well into the valley. We sit on a rock and I chew that stringy jerky from some ratlike rodent. He's hungry enough now to eat some without gagging. We both drink Mollish's tea.

I point to myself and say Lorpas, and he points to himself and says Narlpas.

I say, "I'm going to have to do something with your hair." I gesture. "Hair," I say. I keep talking. "Your hair won't do. It's a little late in the season, but we might meet natives any time even so. I've seen men attacked for less. Well, not very often."

Then I point to him. I say, "From now on you're not Narlpas. Narlpas, ayyaa. You're Jack." I point to me. "And I'm not Lorpas. Ayyaa Lorpas. I'm Norman."

I take a good look at his barrel chest and heavy eyebrow ridges, at that coarse black hair. To the natives, we all look as if from the same family. I say, "We're brothers, and you, my friend, have a speech defect, and though you're most likely just as smart as I am, I'm going to be telling everyone you're a little dim-witted."

After we eat, I rinse his hair in the icy stream to take out the stiffener and tie it back in a ponytail.

First he thought I was going to drown him. Or maybe freeze him. I couldn't make him understand. I said, "Ayyaa. OK, OK." Finally I had to gesture as if to hit him again and he gave up and let me rinse his hair.

Afterwards he smiled. Relieved. Knowing he'd made a mistake about me. He said, "OK, OK," and we both laughed. After that things are different between us. He's still scared—more than scared . . . terrified . . . but at least not of me.

I wish I had scissors. Neither of us will be very presentable. Especially with him in my long underwear (now under the shorts). I still have Ruth's pink razors. When we get closer to a town we'll shave and bathe. After sweating out here in the wild for a couple of weeks, I'm pretty stinky.

I find myself a cane, just the piece of a dead branch, but I'll go a lot faster.

The trail has been following a stream ever since we got into the trees. That afternoon, I stop and catch a fish, make a fire and fry it. Jack refuses to eat it. He prefers another piece of dried rodent. Odd that he manages to eat that without too much of a problem. That doesn't give me much respect for the food back on the homeworld. I think of Allush. I wonder if she likes the food. Nothing worse than alien food. I wonder if there are any good trees for her to climb. I wonder if her clothes and messy hair are as ridiculous there as this man's are here. Well, they are. Even here on this world she'd have had to get a haircut and cleaned up.

I'm tired and depressed. It's not late but I stop. I find a level spot away from the trail and roll out the bedrolls. I like seeing my beautiful world new and fresh as if through Jack's eyes, but I'd much prefer bedding down with Allush and Mollish beside me.

Jack, on hands and knees, examines dirt and pebbles. Plucks at plants. At first he's afraid to touch them but I pull some out to show him it's all right. I say, "Plants," and, "These aren't poison. Not to eat, though, but there's others that are. We'll eat some as soon as I see some good ones." I think it's good for me to keep talking so as to give him a feel for the language.

I wonder if he thinks this whole world is nothing but mountains and forests and hardly any people. I wonder if he thinks wandering around and sleeping on the ground is the usual way.

It's dusk. Animals start coming out. A doe walks right in on us. We sit like stones and watch. I say, "Deer." When I say it, the doe does a double take and runs.

A jackrabbit and a gray fox, come together, stay not three yards apart and don't pay any attention to each other or to us. The jackrabbit is as big as the fox. I say, "Fox and Jackrabbit." And off they go.

He says, "Jack." I say, "Ayy *yaa*. Jack *rabbit*." He says, "OK, OK." I guess we're talking.

He's getting used to being Jack and he calls me Norman. Well, he can't say Rs. The old ones had the same problem. He calls me No man. There's some truth in that.

I show him how to work the flashlight. I put it by his bedroll. Again I say, "Sleep." And he tries to repeat it.

"Not Shleep. Sleep." A logical mistake. Our language is so full of "Sh" sounds. I think: Allush, Allusha, and Mollish.

"OK, OK."

"You know there *is* another word for OK."

I suppose he'd say, Yesh.

"OK, OK."

Does he think it has be said twice to count?

Down here there'll be all sorts of night noises. I hope he isn't frightened . . . or any more scared than he already is.

I WAKE IN THE MIDDLE OF THE NIGHT. BEYOND OUR sheltering tree, I can see the starlit sky and Jack, silhouetted against the dazzle of it, looking up. I watch him watching. I think what he must be thinking, never having seen stars. Odd, I'm feeling so proud of this world, so proud of this sky, though what have I got to do with any of it?

IN THE MORNING WE HAVE A SPECTACULAR SUNRISE. I teach him, "Beautiful." He says it, though for all I know, he thinks it means garish. (It *is* a little overdone.) Or maybe he even thinks it means ugly. Or maybe just means sunrise or colorful or sun. I say, "Sun." I point. I gesture. I draw a circle in the dust. I make a solar system. "Earth. Sun."

Small gray birds flit back and forth with wonderfully complicated calls. I whistle but I can't imitate them. Jack tries, too. We laugh. "Birds," I say. "Bird, birds. One bird, two birds, three birds, four. . . ."

"OK, OK. Bird. Bird sss."

"You got it."

I'VE TAUGHT HIM "SLEEP," "COME," "ONE TWO three four five," "let's go," "thank you," and . . . (and I couldn't help it) I taught him, Yay and Wow. Those were by mistake. Wow is what I said whenever I suddenly came across a spectacular view. Yay is what I say when we see the first houses.

We come to a dirt road, hike a mile down it, and there they are. These are those of the fancy summer people, scattered high in the foothills. This time of year they're empty. Shuttered. Everything turned off. No water, no heat, no electricity.

Jack has been wearing my long underwear under his shorts. He looks too weird for coming into town.

I hate to break into a house and steal—yet again— but I'm already wanted for much more than that. Besides, I'm just going to take a pair of pants and maybe a shirt. Under my sweater my shirt—Ruth's husband's shirt—is little more than rags. It wasn't that good even before they cut the sleeve off to get at my wound.

I have to break into three houses before I find clothes big enough for us. I pry off one shutter and break one window in each house. I teach him, "stay" and the hand signal as if for a dog. I hide him each time behind an arborvitae—almost all the houses have them. I only help him climb in, after I find a house with clothes the right size. I hope he doesn't think this is how we go into houses all the time.

I say, "You may not think so, but there are such things as doors."

Because of the shutters, there's not much light except near the shutter I broke. When I check for clothes, I find a big flashlight. I hand it to Jack. He flashes it around the rooms.

There are big paintings of these very same mountains on the walls. He examines them as if he's never seen such art before. I know our people had carvings because of all those up in the Secret City and then Mother drew pictures for us. How could we not have had paintings? Or maybe they wouldn't have had them of the exact same mountains which are right outside the shutters. That does seem a little odd.

There are lots of photos of the natives . . . on the mantle, desk, tops of bookcases. He brings them to the opened shutter and studies them. All those sharp, smooth faces—so much finer than ours. There are both blonds and brunettes . . . much more variety, even in this one family, than we have among our people.

There are two telephones, two TV sets, radios and CD players but the electricity is off. I don't dare turn it on. Light would shine out from the shutters.

I show him the bedrooms. He bounces on the beds. Lies down. Smiles a big smile as if a good bed is the best thing he's seen on this world so far.

I take the flashlight and leave him on the bed. I find him polypropylene underwear, blue jeans, a sweater. . . . There's a pair of scissors. I'll chop off his hair.

And here are dresses and some loose silky slacks . . . shoes that look . . . at least to me . . . as if for dancing. Jack makes me happy because I see everything with new eyes, but, on the other hand, everything is dulled down because Allush isn't here to see it with me. I'd have taken a dress for her or these loose silky slacks. I wonder what she'd look like in a nice dress and with her hair cut and combed. I wonder what her legs are like not all covered up with leather. And Mollish. . . . I'd have stolen her some polypropylene underwear. Maybe she'd have liked a dress, too, though the way she strode around I doubt it.

When I check on Jack, he's sound asleep, sprawled on the king-sized bed. I leave him be.

There's food in the house. Rice, pasta, flour . . . coffee and tea . . . left in the cupboards from the summer.

I find where the water's turned off and turn it on. The gas is off but I find a little camp stove. I start cooking pasta.

There are no cans or jars of tomatoes, they would freeze, nothing to put on the pasta except some Parmesan.

There's a battery radio. You can only get one station up here in the mountains. I was hoping for news but it's country music.

When the spaghetti is done I wake Jack. Hard to

do. For once he's really sound asleep. Probably for the first time since he's been here. I'd let him sleep, but the pasta will be gummy if it sits too long. Not that he'd know the difference.

By now he's hungry enough to eat some of anything though I can see the stringy spaghetti bothers him. I wish I could explain what it's not.

We sit in the dark kitchen in front of a window where no doubt there's a magnificent view out from behind the shutters.

We listen to the music. The news comes on. An accident on Main Street. A drug arrest. A couple of lost dogs. Which team won the softball game. A storm is coming. Maybe get here by tomorrow night. Jack leans close to listen.

I sleep on the bunk bed in a kids room. He goes back to the master bedroom. In the morning I heat water on the camp stove. We have tea and then we shave using the disposable razors in the house. Even brush our teeth. We wash as best we can without hot water. Then I turn the water back off.

I have a hard time getting him to climb out the window. He doesn't want to leave.

"Ayyaa. Ayy *yaa*."

"I know it's nice, but we can't stay. If the arborvitae are alive, somebody comes by to water and look after things."

"Ayy *yaa*!"

"We have to. And the word you want is, No."

"OK, OK. No."

I pull him from the farthest corner of the bedroom, through the living room. I make the gesture of an uppercut.

"Ayyaa."

I push him out the window and prop up the shutter I broke.

He's presentable: tan floppy hat that looks as if he grew up in these mountains (except he's too pale and puffy though a little better after our days of hiking and him not eating much.) The clothes are all better than anything I could ever afford, fancy farmer's shirt, fancy jeans, navy blue sweater. There's nothing in those houses but expensive things.

"You're dressed all in blue. Blue," I say.

We hike down the dirt road till we come to the paved road to town.

"Road," I say.

"OK, OK."

The first time a car goes by, Jack almost falls over with surprise.

He says, "Yay!" and then "Wow."

I say, "You betcha."

And he says, "You betcha."

"No, it's a car. Car."

"OK, OK. Car. You betcha."

BUT MONEY!

I didn't take any when I left Ruth. I didn't want to have anything to do with it ever anymore. I wanted to get out in the wilds way beyond money. I was hoping my own people have some other way to live than accumulating money. Mother never said. I never asked. I wonder how Allush will get along there on the homeworld without it. Maybe they all get what they need some other way.

But if Jack is going to stay in the Down . . . even for a short time, that's going to take money.

There's a field of cows, brown with white faces. Females with calves.

Jack says, "Yay!" and, "Wow!"

"Cows," I say. "And calves."

I talk. "These are not the kind where milk comes from. Not that you've had any milk. Besides, it will make you sick. It does all of us."

"Kind where shick," he says. Or something rather like it.

He sits on the edge of the ditch by the side of the road and watches. The calves come over and watch him, too. They cavort around, jump and play like all young things do. Jack laughs. He's not so scared anymore. I don't know if that's good or bad. Better that he's scared and careful.

When we get up to leave, the calves, romping, follow us along the fence as far as they can—until they're fenced off. Then they call out after us. Jack yells, "Yay," back at them and makes a little pushing gesture. Is that how they wave good-bye on my world?

We start seeing people. First, in the distance in the

fields, sitting on tractors, harvesting hay and alfalfa. Jack keeps looking at me as though I could tell him about it. I say "Hay smells good," and touch my nose.

Then a girl turns on to the road and walks right past us. Jack yells, "Wow!" even louder and actually stops and stares as she goes by.

"Sorry ma'am. He's feebleminded."

She doesn't answer but hurries past at a trot. I don't blame her.

Jack turns around to watch her leaving.

I say, "Ayy *yaa*! *No*, for heaven's sake! Don't do that!"

I don't know if I get through or not.

But he does it again. This time it's two men. He could get in trouble if he does that to the wrong people. Thank goodness he hasn't done it to a wife walking with her husband.

I push him. I use that sideways push my parents used with me. That's our way. We don't spank or whip like some natives here do. It's never a hard push, but it puts you just a little bit off-balance. You have to step sideways so as not to fall. His parents must have done that to him. He'll know what I mean. Well, maybe not until I do it again at the proper time.

Those men will be thinking we're both crazy. But they go on by. I can see why he stared, and yelled, though. One of those men was like us, big, heavyset, thick features, bumpy forehead, barrel chest. . . . His hair isn't black streaked with red like ours, but completely carrot red. Jack looks at me again.

I say, "Now you see why we can get by on this world."

We're almost at the town. First smaller fields with maybe a couple of goats, then sidewalks begin and rows of little houses, several of them Carpenter's Gothic, colorful, with bobbles and knobs and dowels and pegs. He stops and stares at those in particular.

"Are you thinking these are nice or too much? Actually I like them."

"Actually I. Actually I."

I don't think he has the idea of what makes a word. I point. "I. You." I say again, "I . . . I like them."

"I? I you?"

We walk to the middle of town. There's only one main street. There's people. I have to push him three times before he stops staring at them.

We look in the shop windows. I try to teach more words, but I know it's got be grammar one of these days, too. I keep talking to keep giving him the feel of the language. Also it keeps me busy. If I didn't I'd feel too depressed about Allush.

"Those are shoes; those are dishes and pots and pans, that's a pan like mine; dresses—for women—girls, like that girl you saw. And here's a pair of pants just like yours. . . ."

We still have dried food left, and I took a little

instant coffee from that house. We find a park with a pond and benches, a water fountain. Ducks in the pond. We sit and eat and drink cold coffee out of my one cup. A few other people are picnicking, too. We people-watch and duck-watch. I talk again. "Pond, ducks, bench, people. . . ." And then, "You know we're in danger. There's a man. Well, he's after me, not you. He can talk the home language. You'll be able to talk with him." I say, "Worse luck," and, "I hope never."

If Youpas shaved, cut his hair, and put on native clothes, I'd never recognize him but I'm not any different from what I was. He'll not know that Allush has gone home. There's not a sign of any of us left back on the trail except some burned patches. I wonder what he'll make of those.

"I wish I could ask you if Allush can come back if she changes her mind. When could she come and where? Do I need a beacon so she can home-in on me? Should I go back to the Secret City in spite of Youpas? I wonder what Allush's native name was? I didn't think to ask. I never think to ask anybody anything. Not in time, damn it."

Jack says, "time damn it."

I say, "And here come dogs. Dog. Dog ss."

In town they're mostly fenced in but here in the park some are loose. All my life I've had a problem with dogs . . . or rather some dogs. My people have an alien smell. Most dogs seem to think we're a curiosity they have to keep examining, but some attack—even dogs who've never attacked anybody before. Mother was scared of them. She never let us have any. But I've gotten friendly with some when I had the chance. I wonder, though, there weren't any up in the Secret City . You'd think they'd have come in handy. Allush would have liked them. She said she tamed fox kits. She said she once had a pet raven.

So dogs come sniffing around us. Three. Two are just curious but one won't stop barking. We're disturbing the whole park. I throw out our last piece of dried rat. (I've been calling it that to myself from the start though not out loud to Mollish and Allush.)

A toddler wanders over and stares. I've wondered before if little kids can tell. They always look as if they can. As soon as they can talk, that seems to go away. The kid points at us, says, "Daddy." Toddles closer. He's one of those completely white-headed babies.

Jack stares again. "Don't stare." I gesture as if to push him though the kid doesn't care if he's being stared at or not. In fact the kid is staring, too. Not a good lesson for Jack.

"Do people on our world stare?"

Allush and I. . . . If we couldn't have children of our own, we could adopt some. Maybe. If I had a decent job and identity papers. Unlikely that I ever would have.

Jack is smiling. The kid smiles, too. Jack is starting to relax even though the dogs scared him. The parents of the kid look at us.

I get up. I say, "Let's go."

"OK, OK. Let's go."

I wonder if he thinks we'll have another nice bed tonight. More likely it'll be a hayloft with animals underneath or a garage. Or maybe the back of a truck.

ALLUSH

IN THE MORNING THE BRIGHT LIGHT IS STILL ON BUT not so noticeable. All the dazzle is from outside, and each wall is a window. I slurp myself out of bed and look out. I'm thinking, Wow, wow, wow, and wishing there was somebody to share it with.

I notice there's a mirror I hadn't seen last night. Or did it just appear? A morning thing? I laugh when I see my hair. Short and in all sorts of swirls and designs, parts of it straight and parts of it curly. Because of being in the sun, there used to be lots of bleached red to it but they've colored it a uniform shiny black. My face looks different without my mop of hair. Kind of naked. I've no idea if I'm good-looking or not. I mean for one of my kind. Beautiful Neanderthal? Not back on that world.

One of the men from last night pops out of the elevator without knocking. I think it's one of the same ones from last night though dressed differently. I have a hard time taking him seriously with that hairdo though I know mine is pretty much the same.

He says, "Greetings, greetings," in the home language.

I ask for a drink of water. Now—a little late—he gives me a lesson in the buttons. He says he's sorry, he thought I'd know. He also shows me there's a bed adjustment. (Soft and softer.) There actually is a closet with blankets. And clothes . . . kimono-like clothes . . . in three different sizes. There's a pop-out shower over that depression so I didn't make a terrible mistake when I peed there.

Next to the closet door, there's a bathroom door. It's a tiny room with a hole in the floor. I didn't know those were doors and even if I'd known, I wouldn't have known you had to push inwards first to pop them open outwards.

Then he says the Special wants to talk to me and then gives me a lesson in how to use the elevator.

Once down, I try to look in ground floor windows of what look to me like stores. The man says, "Don't do that."

"But aren't these stores?"

"Yes, but not that kind."

"What kind then?"

I think he says, "For other people." Or maybe,

"Other kinds than you." Anyway not for my kind—
whatever that is.

"What is my kind?"

"That's to be determined later."

That scares me. Is there some sort of caste system
I don't know about? With some people not as good
as others? So low they can't even look in store windows? They had that same kind of things back there
though they tried to pretend they didn't. Worse in
some places than in others. Then I think about how,
except for Mollish who came as a helper, all the
tourists came from wealthy families. Who else could
afford to go? I must have come from a wealthy family. How could I not? Can't they tell that?

They've given me stiff shoes that make me two
inches taller. They hurt. I'm used to moccasins. I
clunk along. I'd rather be barefoot.

"I can't walk far in these foot things." (I forget
their word for shoes.) Now I'm sorry I didn't pay
more attention to our language, but then us kids
wondered if we'd really ever get back home. *Home*!
I always wanted to come here, but I'm not so sure
anymore—not if I'm the wrong kind. Maybe
Mollish was right all this time. She liked it better
back there.

He says, "It's not far, but a swing, if you have a
prefer."

So they call those boat-like porches "swings."
That's what they feel like, too.

"I have a prefer."

So we're raised up again, and, yes, it *is* as if we're hanging by something in the sky, but you can't see what. And then we're arcing down. He sees me looking up, and says, "It's just a. . . ." and then a strange combination of words. "Dust hook," or something of the sort.

Up in a tower again. (But that's all there are.) It's on the thirty-something floor (if I remember my numbers). "Twenty thirteen," I think he said. When Mollish was teaching me my numbers—trying to, that is—she said the natives do that some places too. She said, "You'd think a civilized country, like France and like us, would have changed it a long time ago."

An old man opens the door of the elevator to let us in. I recognize that it's an office. It's full of spools of wires as we would have tapes. Up to the ceiling and on three sides, nothing but these spools and their labels. Unlike the room I was in, there's only one wall that's a window and not even all of that one.

Though he's thin, the man looks soft and weak as they all do. He has the most ridiculous moustache I ever saw or ever thought could be. It curls back and up into his hair. But then I haven't seen many on any world.

He's dressed more simply than anyone I've seen so far except his pants have little pockets just the right size for spools all down the sides and make him look bowlegged. He has a sort of clown hat flopping over one ear, but when he sees me staring at it—I must look shocked—he takes it off. He's bald, with the same little fringe of hair you see on men, both of our kind and on the natives back there.

The young man leaves with an odd gesture that looks as if he's tossing something behind him.

The old man has a nice smile. He says both, "*Buenos dias*," and, "Good morning." Those were the two native languages that our parents learned, though just a little bit of them before they left for their sightseeing trip. They didn't think they'd need much. Mostly they depended on the little phrase books they always carried.

When I say, "Hello," he goes on in English. He says, "I can't really talk those languages all that goodish. Neither one. Let me know if you don't understand. I sorry . . . am. Am I?" Then he laughs. Kind of a giggle.

Right away I feel almost as if I'm back with Lorpas, and I laugh, too, and then I cry again, but just a little. I don't know why I seem to cry every time I laugh.

He notices and hands me a soft paper. They had those back there, too, but I never had one before.

We sit side by side on a too-soft couch next to a low table facing the one clear wall. He takes out a reedy thing, sucks at it, one long suck, and puts it back in his pocket. Then, in our own language, he says, "This right here is Olowpas."

I answer in our language, too, though I know my

accent isn't right. "Does that mean the brightest bird?"

"How nice of you to remember."

"I'm Allush."

"The little blue-moon flower. And, so far I mean, how are you?"

"Fine."

I guess I'm fine.

"*Excellent*!"

You'd think that was the best news he's had all day.

Then he goes back to English, as if what he wants to say is too important to be misunderstood.

"Here's a problem. When you were rescued, two young men were left back by mistake. Those men know nothing of that world and have no homing devices nor are they near any devices so we can't find them. Would you be willing to go back and try? Find? Our last and only noticing of them was when we rescued you."

I start to feel even more trembly than I already do. I start thinking: Lorpas! I wouldn't have to stay back there. Maybe I can get Lorpas to come home with me.

"If we put you back exactly where you were, do you think you could find out and pass them a returning device? Their leader, I say, I say, oh I say, returned dead."

The way he stutters, he's obviously upset about the dead man.

He puts his hand on my arm just like Lorpas often did. I don't know if he's being so sweet as a ploy to get me to agree or if he really is this nice.

Tears start again. He says, "Dear child." Then says it in Spanish, too. "*Querida niña. ¿Mi iha? ¿Miha?* How say it? So, so sorry. This must be so strange and so new to you."

Though all my life I thought I wanted to come back here, and I *am* excited to be here—in a way that is—now, suddenly, I feel a great relief. Yes, back! To Lorpas and Mollish.

"We can put you so very much exactly where you were when we rescued you."

"That was on a narrow scary ledge. Can you get me there in a way I won't fall over the edge?"

"We can be exact."

"I don't know what that means."

"Within a few . . . you call them feet I believe." Then he gestures. "This close."

It sounds chancy. And then clothes. It'll be windy and cold up there. Besides, I can hardly walk in these shoes.

"I'll need shoes. I'll need my old deerskin clothes. And can I get rid of this stuff on my hair before I go?"

I notice he isn't wearing any on his hair and his is a natural white.

"As to hair, not yet. As to clothes, I'm afraid your clothes were destroyed, they were too much contaminated, but we'll get you fitted-out properly."

I don't know what he means by properly.

"I don't want to come dressed for Hawaii or as any kind of tourist."

"No need."

He gets up and brings us both cups with that reddish drink.

"What is this?"

"Aqua. Water. I thought to keep it simple for you at the start."

I don't say anything about how awful the food tasted and how this so-called water tastes funny, too. I like him. I don't want to complain. We sit and sip. We look out towards the one piece of window that's not covered with shelves of spools.

He says, "I just, I just, I just," and waves his hands—that same brushing at flies gesture I saw the people make when I first arrived. "We've been bringing all our people, but they have problems. Of course by now they're all second generation. They have no idea what it's like here. I'm afraid they have a . . . what do you call it? . . . a pink view of our world and the reality is disappointing. We're going to keep them a while longer—let them get used to us, but you. . . . You were there when we lost those two. If you would help get them back? So then you can choose to stay or as you wish."

He gets a bowl and in it there's what looks like fruit.

"Maybe these will be more tasty than. . . ." and

another word I don't know. Does he know I couldn't eat that goo they gave me?

I take a tiny tentative bite. It's like an uncooked quince, hard but not unpleasant. I gnaw at it while he talks and takes another sip from that straw thing.

"Also there's a family. Youpas Youpas and Ush Youpas. The branches of them are anxious for news of all their owns. If there were any children they want them returned. You might look into it. Is that possible on that world? Are there lists and regulations? Those children are. . . ." Another word I don't know. ". . . and would be. . . . " He searches for a word. ". . . special and splendid also if they could be of return. They would have a tower."

"I know someone named Youpas."

I find myself blushing because of my dislike for him. Hate actually, and I worry that it will show. I think right away of our murdered white mule. I worry that this man will think we were lovers because I'm so embarrassed, and that makes me blush even more. If *I'm* going to go back to stay, I'd like nothing better than to have Youpas come to this world.

Used to be, I could shake my hair over my face when I was embarrassed. I shake my head in my old way, but nothing happens to this stiff short hairdo. I try to hide behind my fruit which, of course, is impossible. I take a big bite and concentrate on chewing.

"Good," he says. And says, "And good again. It would be an important welcome to have him back. Perhaps you'd like to stay and rest a day or two and see what's here before you go."

"I think I can rest better back home." There, I said it. I called that place home.

"Come with me and see the sights. Now that we have you, brave person, we want you to know where you come from and perhaps like us enough to want to come back. There's special. Special music and dancing. Special food. Only for my kind."

I like him more and more but I'm worried about myself on this world. I ask him, "What kind? What am I?"

"It doesn't matter, you'll be with me."

"What about when I'm not with you?"

"But you are and will be."

"Are kinds so important?"

Again he waves his hands, brushing flies, and says, "I don't. I just don't. I just."

LORPAS

I PASSED THROUGH THIS SAME LITTLE TOWN ON MY

way north. Even back then I was thinking of heading west to lose myself in the wilds. Maybe look for the Secret City even though I thought it was a myth. We all wanted a retreat just for us. A place where we'd never have to pretend we were them, even though those of us born here are more them than us. I thought the city was just wishful thinking, but after Ruth and that burning, I wanted to get off alone— anywhere, away from everybody. Now I want to get away in the other direction . . . lose myself among the natives, try to forget Allush and the claustrophobic warrens of the Secret City and its useless grand entrances.

But now, and most important, I need to avoid Youpas. In these little towns he'd have no trouble asking if anyone had seen his brother—two brothers now—and surely somebody would have remembered me and Jack. We sat in the park long enough for half the town to see us.

The valley is a flat desert with mountains on both sides. Ruth told me it was four hundred miles of valley, never wider than ten miles across. Only two ways out, north and south, above or below the mountain ranges. This town is in the middle.

We're pretty well dressed now, especially Jack, and we have our backpacks so we look like hikers just coming off the mountains. The natives always pick up hitchhikers that look like mountain climbers. I hope Jack behaves himself.

WE'RE PICKED UP BY A PICKUP TRUCK PULLING A big trailer full of horses.

There's a teenage girl and a man in the cab. He has one of those handlebar mustaches that's in style in the west—black, streaked with gray. He has to lean across the girl to talk to us.

"You'll have to ride in the truck bed and we're only going as far as Big Pinetree. Is that OK?"

While I'm busy thinking: Pinetree is only a half hour down, and about as big as one gas station, it's Jack says, "OK, OK. Let's go."

He's getting too comfortable. And the way he stares at the girl. . . . He's going to get himself in trouble.

She *is* a beautiful example of their kind. Blond—almost white hair, smooth, oval face, blue eyes, sharp features—one of those pixie faces. She ducks her head, shy, and gives Jack a little pixie smile. She's about as opposite of our women as a native girl could get. Even more opposite because she's still a child. You can just see the beginnings of breasts under her T-shirt. I can understand why Jack stares.

Then he turns and points at the horses and says, "What's that?" Of course it comes out, "Whash shat?"

The whole upper section of the trailer is windows so you can get a good view. There are five horses in it along with some bales of hay. The horses look out at us. One whinnies. Jack jumps back.

The man sticks his head farther across the girl to

get a better look at Jack. Jack stares back at him. No doubt it's that handlebar mustache or maybe the cowboy hat. Jack's expression is bland. He does look feebleminded.

I say, "It's OK, he's harmless." (I hope he is.) "My brother's retarded."

The man frowns, but if we're in the back of the truck it shouldn't bother him too much. He says, "Well . . . I guess," and we hop in.

Jack is beginning to enjoy himself. I felt safer when he was terrified.

I say, "For heaven's sake it's horses. Horses! And keep your mouth shut." I put my hand over my mouth. "No talking. Ayy *yaa* talking." Then I put my hand over his mouth. I make the motion of my uppercut. "No!"

"OK, OK."

"And for heaven's sake don't keep saying OK twice all the time. What am I going to do with you?"

He doesn't look scared at all, he looks happy to be riding in the back of a truck. When he got in he banged on the metal side hard, three times as if to test what it's made of. As we drive, he sits with his head out the side, looking forward like a dog enjoying the wind. I wonder what I can do to terrify him again, or at least scare him enough to shut him up. Maybe a horse could do it. Maybe a nice electric shock. But I don't know enough about the home-world to know what might work. Could be something silly and little, a spider or a mouse. I wouldn't wish a snakebite on him, but some kind of bite that hurts a lot but doesn't kill would be perfect.

But this man might have some work for me so I could make a little money without stealing for a change. There'll be these bales of hay to help with, maybe mucking out stalls. . . . I've worked with horses. I can curry them, hose 'em down, pick their hooves. . . . When they let us off at Big Pinetree I'll ask.

The man will think it odd that a couple of hikers in pretty good outfits (at least Jack is well dressed) are looking for odd jobs. Me. . . . I look pretty much like somebody who'd be looking for work.

I have about as many identity documents as a wetback. I've driven trucks, but never legally.

I wonder if Jack has been trained not to use the freeze. I wonder if, back on the homeworld, they'd use it at the slightest excuse. Would it be an automatic reflex whenever in danger? Except he didn't use it on me when he thought I was drowning him.

Before we get to Big Pinetree I make Jack turn away from the wind and look at me. I make that uppercut gesture again. I gesture talking. I gesture stay behind me. I gesture be quiet. I don't know if any of it gets through.

When the man stops at the edge of town to drop us off, I tell Jack, "Stay," with the same gesture as for a dog that I used before. I get out to talk to the man about getting work. I tell him I know how to work with horses. I tell him my brother will be pretty much useless but he won't hurt anybody.

Actually, I can't be sure of that. My parents never thought the natives were worth much consideration, and then look what they did to Ruth. Jack might even be one of them that burned us. I hope I can keep an eye on him.

The man does have work. Turns out there's a half-dozen bales of hay in the back of the trailer behind the horses. I jump back in with Jack and the man drives out to the far side of town, towards the mountains. Big barn, little house. Of course there's a dog and she goes crazy. Especially with Jack. Jack backs up until he's against the side of the pickup.

The man and the girl keep calling, "Elizabeth Alice, Elizabeth Alice." The man says his daughter named her and insists she be called the whole thing.

Finally the girl grabs the dog, takes her up and shuts her in the house.

I say, "That always happens with my brother. He's been away in a home. He must smell funny. Or it could be they can smell that he's feebleminded."

Then I and the girl lead the horses out to pasture while the man moves the tractor to make a place for the bales. Jack watches. Thank goodness the horses do scare him. He sees how a couple throw their heads and paw the ground if they're not the first to be led out. He sees how we have a hard time holding a couple of them till we get them through the gate. Three other horses have come to meet them. They all whinny to each other and then trot off, two by two.

But Jack is mostly watching the girl. Easy to see he's fallen in love at first sight. Or fallen into fascination. I can't imagine what he's thinking. Is she ugly to him or beautiful? Looks like beautiful—worse luck.

Her father... odd that he's so dark and she's so fair... keeps a good watch on Jack.

The man and I move the bales over near the barn and cover them with a tarp. Jack tries to help, but he can't even lift one. He sits on a pile of three tires— that's their mounting block—and watches, not looking ashamed or apologetic. Is that normal for my people? But good: He seems more and more feebleminded.

The man gives me a look.

I shake my head. "I know, he's in bad shape. I was hoping our hike would help. At least he's better than he was a few days ago. I think he's lost ten pounds out in the woods."

(And that, not only from the hiking, but from hardly daring to eat anything.)

The girl does everything except lift bales. I'll bet she's hardly fourteen. She unhitches the trailer and drives the truck up to the house. Then comes back to put the ramp up and close the horse trailer.

Jack stares at her the whole time.

I say, "Sorry. I can't stop him staring. He was in an institution for years until I took him out. Everything is new to him." (That's one true thing at least.)

After we finish, we sit on a couple of bales and

talk and the man smokes a cigar. We watch the color fade on the eastern mountains.

Jack can't get over the smoking. He keeps looking at me for some kind of answer. I say, "It's OK," and he says, "Wow," as loud as I did back in the mountains when I saw a good view.

Jack looks like he wants to try it. The man asks me if he should give him one. I say, "He'll set the bales on fire or worse."

The girl is Emily and the man is Corwin. He and his daughter do all the work, mostly alone except for neighbors' help now and then. But Emily is in junior high school and doesn't have much time these days.

I make up a bunch of half-truths about Jack. How we haven't had any time together until now. How I took him out of the home because I thought he'd do better having adventures with me. And he *is* doing better. A lot. He's talking some which he didn't do at all before. How he's never hurt anybody. What I hope for him: more talking, more physical work, adventures that will open the world to him. How I want him to be able to make money on his own. How I think dogs know . . . can smell his disabilities like Elizabeth Alice did.

I like Corwin and I think he likes me.

He hands me a fifty dollar bill. I say, "That's too much for just a couple of hours," and he says, "There's more work in the morning," and asks if we want to bed down in the barn. Then he invites us to supper. At first I think, we shouldn't. This will be the first time Jack sits down at a table with plates and forks and spoons to deal with. I was hoping to start him off on all that when we were alone.

There's a lady there, looks after the house and does the cooking but she's not the wife and mother. She only works there a couple of days a week and goes home in the evening. She looks at Jack with even more suspicion than Corwin does.

At the table, and thank goodness, Jack watches us and does everything slowly. He's so awkward with a knife and fork he really does look feebleminded. He spills stuff as if he was a two-year-old.

They have rice, meatloaf, peas. The rice shocks him almost as much as the spaghetti did. He studies the peas. Takes one apart. He won't eat anything but the meatloaf. He doesn't trust the chocolate cake either. Sniffs at it and then makes a disgusted face.

Emily says, "How can he not like chocolate?"

The woman gives him an apple. He does like that but eats the whole thing, seeds and stem, too.

Strange, Emily is as fascinated with him as he is with her. She can't keep from giggling and then she looks at me and says, "Sorry."

I say, "It's OK." I say, "Jack thinks rice is maggots."

She giggles again. Jack has an absolutely perfect feebleminded grin on his face.

"See? He doesn't mind."

That storm the radio spoke of last night has

arrived. We—all of us—sit on the front steps just under the overhang and watch it come. We can't see the snow-capped mountains behind us, the foothills are in the way, but in front of us, across the valley, are the rounder mountains. We watch the lightning hit trees over there. Every now and then we see a burst of fire and then it dies. The air is too thin up there for fires to get started.

Jack has learned Wow perfectly. Emily says it, too, and pretty soon they're both saying, "Awesome," and "Outta sight." They both sound like teenagers. Jack says, "Aayy yaa," now and then, as if it doesn't just mean no. I guess we might say no that way, too, sometimes.

And the smell of wet sage! I take a deep breath. I say, "Smells good. Say it Jack."

"Shmell good."

Emily says, "Say, It stinks."

"Shtink."

I keep thinking, My world! It even smells good. I hope Jack will at least understand why some of us want to stay here.

Later we spread our sleeping bags on the prickly hay in the loft. Jack looks disappointed. He says, "Bed?" I say, "No, no beds this time." He says, "Aayya." But he's resigned.

I squash all the spiders I see. I try to pantomime bites. I show him the webs.

"Some of these are really bad."

He doesn't look scared.

I pinch his arm hard enough to raise a welt. "Bad bite!"

"OK, OK."

At least he doesn't try to pinch me back.

In the morning, the sandy patch in front of the barn is all mud. Jack's fancy waterproof hiking boots are perfect. Taking those really was stealing. They probably cost, maybe a hundred and fifty dollars and are hardly worn at all. My worn-out shoes aren't much good for anything anymore. I should have stolen something for myself. Just about anything would be better than these—though I'd have to do something about raising the heel on my bad foot.

At breakfast Jack is already better at managing a knife and fork. I'm afraid he won't seem so moronic if he learns so fast. We'll be in trouble—all of our people will be—if anybody thinks we're some sort of aliens. But our people did get along, all these many years, without being discovered, and then no rational native would believe in us even if we told them exactly where we're from. Just so we don't break a leg. Our bones are so much thicker, especially our males'.

Corwin asks, would we stay a few more days and help bring the cows down from the hills. Emily would have to miss school if we can't do it— fifty dollars a day and all our food—which will be beans.

I tell him if I can bring Jack along and if there's an old nag that's big enough for him, then yes, we'd like to. At least I'll have a few days without straps pulling on my sore shoulders.

Jack is going to think all sorts of odd things about this world. He's seen planes passing overhead and their jet streams and he ought to experience a city, except I can just see us in some one-room hovel with bathroom down the hall, paper-thin walls and noisy neighbors. That would be all we could afford. Makes me think of my growing up years. No wonder Mother wanted to go home.

I'm worried, though, because now we'll be heading back to those same mountains, and who knows where Youpas has got himself to. But we do need money or we can't get anywhere. Can't even eat.

I wonder if Youpas is in town now and if he's been asking for a big ugly lug that looks like him. Wonder what he'll think when he hears there's two of us.

Maybe, if we're out cavorting in the woods yelling to the cows, there'll be time for Youpas to simmer down some. Though from what Allush said about him, he never simmers down. She said they used to call him Chicago because they think big city people are always violent. Like lots of country folk, they distrust anybody from a city.

Jack is definitely in love. Emily likes him, too. She thinks he's funny. She likes to make him laugh. Next morning she brings out her little plastic horse. Jack's whole face lights up. He says, "Outta sight." I guess I don't have to worry quite yet that he doesn't seem feebleminded enough.

Emily gives the plastic horse a big sloppy kiss.

Jack points at her and says, "You. . . . You, yay."

She ducks her head, suddenly shy, but pleased.

I can't think why she likes him. Maybe she knows her father wouldn't want her to. Maybe she likes how inappropriate he is for her to like. Or maybe she knows he's safe since nothing can ever happen between them because it's so wrong that she wouldn't even really want it herself.

She turns to Corwin, takes the cigar out of his mouth, says, "You know you shouldn't." And then, "Dad, I want to go with you. You were going to let me before these men came. Besides I already told everybody I was going to miss school for a few days. I even did my homework ahead of time. Can't I come? Why should you have all the fun?"

But Corwin says, "Absolutely not. Why do you think I asked them? It's for you . . . so you don't have to miss school."

"*Daddy*!"

But it's, "No," no matter what she says—and she says a lot. Could be, too, Corwin doesn't want Emily and Jack to be together any more than necessary.

So she goes off to school, grumpy, (her black cow-boy-hat low over her eyes, and jeans low, too, so her belly button shows. I wonder what Jack thinks of that. Well, everything is new.)

We load the pickup with food and tack, catch the

horses and, finally, take off. Jack and I are in the back of the truck again and the trailer is full of horses. This time six so we each have two, and this time with the dog. It's not only Emily that's fascinated by Jack, but the dog, Elizabeth Alice, too. She hovers around Jack more than around me. There must be an even odder smell to someone who grew up on the homeworld, ate the homeworld food. . . . But she's so happy to be about to do the work she was born for that she's even happy to be with Jack. Mother was wrong, dogs can get along with us just fine.

I keep on teaching Jack. "Truck, saddle, airplane . . . in the sky. Sky." I even work a little on writing. Mostly signs we see on our way out of town. Bar, Restaurant, but also . . . in case he needs it, Men, Ladies, Women (though around here it's frequently Heifer and Bulls or some such). And then, "Soon enough there'll be beans. I hope you don't mind eating them because that's all there's going to be."

He repeats things he knows already, showing off what he remembers. "Tree, treesiz; house, housiz; grass, grassiz; sand, sandiz; one two three four five six. . . ." All the esses sounding more sh than ss.

Talk about feebleminded.

I say, "Pretty good."

Being with Emily even that little bit, has made his language learning much faster.

Jack looks proud of himself, says, "Yup, awe-some."

Soon the road is little more than bumpy ruts in the sand. We raise a great cloud of dust. "Dust."

"Dust. Dustes."

"Just plain dust."

Corwin parks at a dead end, where there's a little oasis of trees and we bring out the horses, hobble them and let them go where they can hop. There's a corral there big enough for a pretty good-sized herd. We cook our beans and bacon, then bed down, all three of us, in the back of the truck.

I know we're near where Jack and I came down from the mountains. Easy to tell by the white-topped peak that was in view then at the same angle as it is now. I hope Youpas has already passed by. Surely he won't think Jack is me and shoot him right off.

NEXT MORNING HERE'S EMILY, SQUATTING BY THE campfire, coffee and oatmeal already made. She rode all night. Her pony is exhausted. She'll have to take one of our extra horses to go help get cows.

Corwin looks both disgusted and resigned. He gets a lot quieter. Thanks her for the coffee with more politeness than necessary. Practically bows as she hands it to him. He squats down, sipping it, and stares into the fire.

●   ●   ●

IT'S NOT AS HARD GETTING JACK UP ON A HORSE AS I thought it would be. That's because Emily does it. He's eager to do whatever she wants him to.

I'm so used to never seeing my own kind. I didn't realize how young he probably is. He might not be much more than twenty himself. Of course I can never ask him. Years on our world are different. I've been here all my life and I don't remember how they figured on our world, so even when Jack gets his numbers straight I can't ask him in any way that I'd understand. And I can't tell him how young Emily is either.

We adjust his stirrups. Emily tells him, "Don't pull. It hurts the horse."

"Horsh."

"Hang on to this knob if you need to. Steer like this." All this mostly with gestures.

But I'm afraid he's going to be more trouble than he's worth. I try to tell him to stick with me, but who he sticks with—of course—is Emily.

He watches, bounces along (I pity the poor horse) and pretty soon he *is* a little help. Thank goodness the horse knows what to do. And Emily is a good teacher. Jack does everything she says as soon as he understands it.

They're both yelling, "Ayy *yaa*," at just about everything that happens, or at nothing. I can just see Emily's whole high school class saying it by next week. Though Ayy yaa is pretty much what we've always yelled at the cows.

Later Emily trots up to me and says, "I don't think he's dumb at all."

I was afraid of that. I say, "I'm glad I took him out with me. It's good for him to be with normal people. And, Emily, you're the best teacher so far."

At lunch, Jack falls down when he dismounts and he can hardly walk. I forgot that always happens. He'll have to sit the afternoon out. I put him in the one and only shady spot, under a wild peach bush on a knoll, so he can watch us.

I wish I could tell him about Youpas. We've been a noisy bunch—actually a *happy* noisy bunch— all along. That worries me because, if Youpas is on the trail above us, he might come to take a look—though why would he think I'd be working cows? Except I'm still wearing Ruth's husband's soft hat. I should have stolen a new one when I had the chance.

But Corwin hasn't been so happy. He's been quiet ever since Emily appeared. He's been ultra-gracious to her... not that he wasn't before. I noticed from the first that he treated her with a kind of concern, as if she was precious and fragile. Now there's this mock gentility added to it. His way of being angry.

Emily avoids his eyes. She looks properly remorseful (even as she's enjoying herself), as if this ultra graciousness is punishment enough.

Next morning we have thirty-four cows rounded up and we start down. Ten are lost up there but

Corwin wants to get down in a hurry. He says he wants to get Emily back to school but maybe what he really wants is to get her away from Jack.

Now, sore as he is, Jack has to get back on a horse. There's no other way. He's not afraid of much of anything anymore. I'm still thinking about how to find a way to keep him scared, and then it happens by itself. The horse steps into a ground-hornet's nest and bucks Jack off. Both the horse and Jack get stung.

I guess I should have taught him, "Run," and, "Jump in the river," a long time ago.

I lope up beside him while Emily gallops after the horse. I jump off, grab him, and run him to the river. It's a little river, about twelve feet wide and a foot deep, but if we lie down we can get covered. The cold will help to take away the pain. Besides these hornets aren't that vicious. By the time we're wet they're gone.

We sit on the bank and I examine his welts. Jack looks petrified again. Good! I suppose he wonders if they've killed him—poisoned him some way. Good! He looks at me, again, as if I'm his only hope and as if I have all the answers . . . which I do.

I say, "You're fine. I know it hurts but you'll be OK."

I think. I've heard some of the old ones died from such things. I take his pulse. That scares him, too. I say, "You're OK. OK, OK." But I'll watch him closely for a while. I say, "Hornets. There's bees and spiders and rattlesnakes and poison ivy. I'm glad you're scared."

Emily trots over with our horses.

Jack is limping and his ankle is starting to swell up. I'll call it a sprain because Mother said, "Never let any doctors see you." She said, "Who knows what the natives of this world would do when they find out about our world and how to get there. They'd try to take over when they see how much better our world is than theirs. After all," she said, "We have oil and minerals, gold, diamonds. Everybody knows what these people did in South America and Africa. North America, too. Wherever they go they're an infestation."

Corwin has a first-aid kit. He tapes up Jack's ankle like a man who's used to doctoring. He even has some stuff for the bites. He puts it on the horse's bites, too.

We get back to work, push all the cows into the corral and sit down to beans and bacon. Cold beans and bacon.

Emily will drive the truck to our next camp site. She'll keep driving it as long as we're on back roads, then Corwin will take over. We should have the cows down in Corwin's pastures on the outskirts of town in one more day.

I'm feeling pretty good, we're earning money—even Jack is a help—and we're staying away from people while he learns more about how to behave. He's properly terrified again, and we're staying away from Youpas. Maybe. There's no way somebody on the trail wouldn't have seen us below them and heard us but we look like anybody else would look, out gathering cows.

ALLUSH

THE WIND ALMOST BLOWS ME OVER THE EDGE. I sit down and try to orient myself. How can it be so much colder here already? How many days has it been? I've lost track.

The weather's often bad this high. Now there's a light pricking snow or, rather, tiny hail splinters, coming sideways, but the air smells *so, so* good. I never realized how good this air was. I never noticed it. I catch some of the little bits of hail in the palm of my hand and lick them up. I feel as if I've been thirsty for days. I haven't really eaten for a long time either. All I did was nibble on that fruit. I hope it was a fruit. Even when Olowpas took me out for a fancy dinner and music, I didn't like anything, especially not smelly fermented. . . . They called it "fermented water" but how can that be? Except maybe with that odd taste and rusty color, it does ferment. But I didn't even like to see Olowpas drinking it. He laughed at me. I think I was his entertainment for the evening. I began to wonder about the real reason he brought me there. It began to be pretty obvious I wasn't the "right kind," or at least, as he said, my status hadn't been determined yet. Olowpas, clearly, thought he was doing me a *big* favor, bringing me to this fancy place, and getting me the right clothes for it. He even gave me a lesson in how to walk and told me not to smile at anybody but him, not to nod my head, and not to blow my nose or wipe my eyes even if I cried, and to keep my hands away from my face. He should have given me a lesson in the food probes. I tried to hold them as he did. We both laughed at that.

When they first saw me at that fancy place, a lot of the people made that same gesture I'd seen at the beginning—as if brushing away flies. I asked Olowpas what that was all about. He tried to tell me, but he used words I'd never heard before. I don't think he wanted me to know.

I didn't understand the music and the dancing at all. It seemed random, and the voices were so artificially high and squeaky. Olowpas said it was very subtle, very intellectual—that it takes a long time . . . "Of knowing and schooling on it. Study, I think you'd say, to appreciate." I felt more of a barbarian than ever. He told me: "Watch the dancer's fingers and foreheads. Watch the little dip of the knees. Count beats. That's fifteen, sixteen, and now back to one again. . . ." I still couldn't see anything to it. My parents used to say how funny and primitive everything was back on that other world—how they had to try hard not to laugh at their dancing and their music and their idea of what was food. I had that same problem there. I had a hard time not laughing, it seemed so silly. I can understand, now, why my parents longed for their homeworld just as I feel more comfortable back where I was born.

At least I'd figured out the bed by that time. I had a good sleep.

I have a little pack with three homing devices. They're smaller than they used to be. My new one is just under my skin in my earlobe, and it's no bigger than a grain of rice. I have others for Lorpas and the two men. I carry them in a sort of locket around my neck. It even holds the tiny pointers for inserting them.

Now I sit, head up, mouth open, tongue out . . . like I used to do when I was a little kid. After doing that for a while, I lick where the hail splinters have settled in the folds of my dry-suit.

Then I realize I'm freezing. I miss my thick mop of hair. Sometimes, when the wind was really bad, I held it over my face with my teeth. This stiff stuff on it makes me all the colder. Olowpas wouldn't let me wash it out there. He said I'd have to wait till I got back here. He said it was important though he never said why.

This is a terrible season to be up here, but it's the right place. There are burn marks on the ledge right next to me. I hope nobody else got hurt besides that one dead man. But there's no way I can study these marks now. I have to get off this ledge until the wind stops blowing.

I hug the high side of the cliff and go back the way we came. I find a sheltering tree where I can wait out the storm. I wonder if all this hail and wind will wash away more signs of what happened.

I curl up with those "hot bars" they gave me. They have things like that here, too, but we never had any. Mother talked about them all the time. She also talked about those socks with batteries. She hated the Secret City because she was always cold, but she saw to it I was warm. Actually mostly too warm.

Except for my head, I'm dressed right for this storm. They gave me a dry-suit, thin and soft. They couldn't give me anything that might reveal to the natives that we were aliens so this suit is not unlike their underwater suits here. They gave me some emergency food—that terrible-tasting paste. Every time I try to force myself to eat some, I don't care how hungry I am, I stop. Then I get hungrier and try again but I can't. Olowpas didn't think I'd get sick from it nor from the water back there because they gave me pills for that when I was in that cell. I thought, Thanks a lot, but I didn't say it, but, well, I guess, yes, thanks a lot.

What if they sent me back here alone because I'm one of the kind of people that doesn't matter? What if I'm a peasant or an untouchable of some sort and everybody has to make that brushing-away flies gesture when I'm around? I know I have no education. That's another reason I don't matter. All I know is what my parents and Mollish...especially Mollish...taught me. Mollish was a good teacher, though. If I'd listened, and read the books (we did have lots of books), I could have learned just about everything there is to learn. I wonder what Lorpas thinks about no education or only as much as I got when I wasn't looking at the ceiling. I wonder how much education he has.

I can die trying to find these two men and nobody cares. Well, Mollish does. She loves me in spite of how I behaved. (Except I've changed.) And Lorpas. Does he? Not enough to follow me back there. I can't wait to tell Mollish that she was right about that world...that I'll believe everything she says from now on. And I have so many things to tell Lorpas. I really don't care if I ever find those two men. Except I did promise to try.

The storm lasts the whole night, but the morning is bright and clear. I go back to the ledge and search for signs of what happened. I see more burn marks and signs of someone going over the side— torn pieces of cloth and what looks like a whole chunk of skin and spots of blood where they went over. What if Lorpas is down there dead or wounded? What if he's been lying here all this time while I was back there having a fancy dinner and a concert?

I scramble—mostly fall and skid—down the scree. I leave bits of the dry-suit on the rocks. It's not very strong. I find two bodies at the bottom. They're already eaten past recognition, but I recognize the clothes. Mollish is hardly there anymore. Her red-streaked hair is still in its neat bun. Part of her is dragged away. I can't look.

Then I look. I want something to remember her by, but there isn't anything I can take without moving her. Then I think, her scarf because it's partly off already and I don't have to touch her. And then I think, this is Mollish. My Mollish! I touch. I put my hand on her arm . . . the bone of her arm. Then I hold what's left of her hand. (The other arm and hand are dragged away.) I sit with her. I talk to her. I apologize for not learning more of what she wanted to teach me. I apologize for running around climbing trees when she needed help. Then I put on her scarf. She knit that herself. It smells of death, but that's not just anybody's death.

Another dead person is close by. Hardly anything left of him either, but clothes and bones. There's one of those tubes they use to return us with, partly covered up with scree. I cover it with even more scree. Olowpas was worried about those getting in the hands of the ignorant natives. They could harm each other, but I don't know what else to do with it right now. And who would be out here, having fallen down in exactly this spot?

I look all around at the bottom of the cliff, but Lorpas isn't here, thank goodness.

I climb back to the trail and sit with my back to the wall. I don't know which direction to go. What would I have done if I were Lorpas and found me gone?

On the mountain across the way I can see three waterfalls rushing down. I remember seeing them as we were crossing the ledge back then. I remember being happy. I sit. I watch a red-tail soar out from right above me. I think: Mollish, look! I forget she's dead even as I'm mourning for her.

Finally I cross the ledge and go on towards the Down. Maybe Lorpas left me some sign. I'm a good tracker, but I don't find anything. I guess the storm washed everything away.

Then I think: Wouldn't Lorpas and that other man . . . if that man is with him . . . wouldn't they want to get back to the Secret City to be near all those beacons? Maybe Lorpas changed his mind and wants to go home where he thinks I am. Then those homers are the only way.

I sat around so much it's already late. I camp in a nice spot. I wrap Mollish's scarf around me. It doesn't smell so bad anymore, now it smells more of weather and of pine forest. Or I've gotten used to it. To death.

There's stars! I never thought about how nice it is

to have them. I always thought a lot of shiny dust and two moons would be better, especially with each moon a different color, but one's enough if you like stars.

I don't know what to do. There's no way I can find the men if they're already somewhere out in civilization. Though . . . maybe . . . since we all look so odd. . . . I can go to all the little towns and ask. Olowpas gave me money. I think quite a bit, though what do I know, we didn't use money up at the Secret City.

Except I don't know the way in either direction. For the whole first part I was just enjoying being with Lorpas. I'll have to blaze a trail as I go so I can backtrack on myself if I need to.

LORPAS

EMILY HAS DRIVEN THE TRUCK TO OUR NEXT camping spot. Then she rode her pony back to us and helped push the cows to where she parked. There's another corral there but hardly any shade this time, so we sit in the shade of the truck. Jack wets his kerchief from our canteen, takes off his hat, and wipes his face and neck exactly like I do. Our hats are on the ground beside us when . . .

(Jack has been wearing a big black cowboy hat Corwin lent him. It's just like Emily's. Mine's just that old floppy hat that belonged to Ruth's husband. I'm leaning back wondering if I'll be able to pry Jack loose from that hat when the time comes to give it back. Or maybe Corwin will let me buy it when we get paid. Or maybe there's one just like it in town.)

. . . when, whoosh, here comes an arrow—swishing past me so close I feel the rush of air. On it goes, into Jack. Not into, just streaks a bloody line across his cheek, captures a piece of his ear, and twangs into the ground beyond us. *Almost* a very good shot.

As with all face wounds, there's a lot of blood.

We all . . . Corwin and Emily, too . . . duck down and after that we look for a good place to duck to, but there aren't any, any better than where we already are.

I stand up and show myself, my hands out and up in a gesture of surrender. "Youpas, Youpas, I'm the one you want. This is Narlpas. He's stranded here from Betasha. Don't shoot him."

Now I've done it. What kind of funny names are these? And where is Betasha? Will Youpas think he has to kill Corwin and Emily now to keep our secret safe?

His next arrow swishes right by me.

But Corwin has a pistol I didn't know about. He shoots all six shots, no questions asked, into the sagebrush in the direction where the arrows came from. I rush to the bushes. Youpas lies—flat on his back. At first I think he's got to be dead or hurt and I go to help, but he kicks up at me. I notice he takes care not to glance into my eyes in case I freeze him again.

I easily outfight him. I'm larger and, as a vagrant and a bum and now and then in jail, I've fought lots of times before. By the time Corwin comes up I've got Youpas in a half nelson.

Corwin was shooting blind. Not a one of his shots hit. I'm thinking it would have been nice if he'd have wounded Youpas just a little bit.

Youpas looks exactly as he did before . . . like the wild mountain man he is . . . all in hand-sewn dearskin with odd designs all over it. His hair, like Allush's, is a tangled mop, as is his beard. (Was he thinking of coming into town like this?)

In spite of how he looks, Corwin says, "Looks like another brother." We're clearly two . . . or rather three now, of a kind.

I say, "Yes," at the same time that Youpas says, "No."

We're too similar for Corwin not to believe me instead of Youpas.

I put more pressure on Youpas' neck and he says, "Yes."

Narlpas and now Youpas? And I yelled Youpas

twice. I say, "This is Hugo." It sounds a little like Youpas. It's the best I can do on the spur of the moment. "Another one of us Norths."

Corwin is concentrated on the job at hand, as usual—in this case untying a lead rope from a halter so as to tie up Youpas—but Emily always pays attention and she's sharp. She'll have noticed I called Jack, Narlpas. And she won't forget I shouted, Youpas, and that now I call him Hugo.

She looks at us as if she suspects all sorts of weird things. Besides, what she has liked about Jack from the start is his strangeness. And now here's one of us, clearly same family, shooting at the others of us, with, of all things, a bow and arrow, and here I am, presumably the older brother (the only one with graying temples) trying to keep everybody in line. Here's Jack, a not-so-dumb dummy, young, but too stocky and thick to look young to them. And I yelled, He's from Betasha. You don't say that about one brother to another.

At least I'll be able to communicate with Jack. That is, if Youpas will cooperate—but what makes me think he will?

Corwin ties up Youpas' hands while Emily, looking more motherly than you'd think a thirteen-year-old could, bandages Jack's face and ear.

Corwin says we'll take Hugo to the police as soon as we get back.

"Let me talk to him. I can persuade him to go back to the mountains where he belongs."

But Corwin doesn't think he belongs anywhere except locked up. I know he's right, but I can't let that happen. Trying to kill people . . . it won't be at all like me being in jail a few days for vagrancy.

"I'll get him out of here as soon as we move the cows."

Corwin gives me that contemplative look of his. I can practically see the thoughts turning around inside his head. Without us he and Emily will have to take the cows down alone and then Corwin will have to ride back for the truck and trailer. On the other hand, here's three big guys wearing out his horses, one is dangerous, and one is smitten with his daughter. On yet another hand he likes me and, in a way, he likes Jack. But another hand, Emily is a tough, capable girl. On the other hand she's his only child.

"I'll keep him in line."

"You have a lot to keep in line."

"I'll manage."

He reloads the pistol and tucks it in his belt. Actually, even though Youpas is one of my own kind, I feel better that Corwin has it handy.

Corwin tells me he'll pay us double for these last days because Jack is doing a good job, but when we get back, he wants us all out of there. Pronto.

"Will do."

If we don't get out of there fast, for sure Corwin will go to the police.

I see Emily taking it all in. I wouldn't be surprised

if she started getting right answers. She's young enough not to have a lot of preconceived ideas of what's logical. She won't think it's crazy to believe in aliens. I know, from my growing up on the outskirts of the native's lives, that country kids know just as much as any city kid.

Meanwhile Jack and Youpas are talking home-talk and I've no idea what they're saying. The language has always sounded odd even to me and especially so now when I think of Emily and Corwin listening. But lots of native languages sound just as odd . . . some full of clicks and glottal stops and grunts. Sniffs and snorts shouldn't seem any stranger. But I should have been having Jack teach me our language instead of trying to teach him the language of the natives. I wonder whose side Jack will be on now.

I say . . . I shout it, "Allush has gone home."

I'm telling Youpas that to shut them up. I know that'll stop him and it does. He deflates. He's stand-ing by the truck. Now he collapses—squats down and leans against a back tire. Doesn't look like a threat anymore. His, "Ay yaaaa," is a wail. (Seems Ayyaa can stand for most anything.) He really does care about Allush.

At first he can't speak. He stares at the ground in front of him as if it takes a while for him to under-stand. Finally he says, "How?"

"You know she wanted to go."

"But all our beacons are back there."

We're talking softly, but not so softly that Emily couldn't hear if she wanted to.

"She stole mine. Narlpas doesn't have one. I don't think. You can ask him, I can't. He'd be snatched back by now if he had one."

But he's too upset to talk. I bring him a tin cup of water and squat down beside him. His hands are tied in front, but he can manage the cup though it's awkward.

"Wouldn't it be better for you to go up to the Secret City? Wouldn't that be where she'd come back to? If she can come back? She might come back."

But he won't be cheered.

"I think she'll find out she liked it here more than she thought she did."

I don't say I'm hoping she'll come back because of me. Maybe she's waiting for me up at the city right now, wondering why I haven't come. But could I find my way back there by myself anyway? Could Youpas even? Much easier to come *out* from the mountains as we did and end up somewhere on the big main road than to go *into* the mountains and end up at a small hidden city.

Corwin cooks bacon and then heats the beans in the bacon fat. Emily watches, squatting by the fire in exactly the same position her father is in. A cowboy position. Jack squats, too, as if he's trying to learn how to be a native.

Youpas won't eat anything, only drinks. Corwin says he'd have brought juice cartons if he'd known Emily was coming. He says, "Maybe Hugo would have liked juice."

Corwin can see Youpas isn't the same man he was a half hour ago. He puts his pistol back under his shirt.

This time Corwin and Emily sleep in the bed of the truck. The rest of us (us "brothers") are around the dying fire, Youpas' lead rope tied around my wrist. I don't like this much. I won't sleep very well. If he blames me for everything that's happened, he'd be right. If I was him I'd kill me first and then go back to the Secret City to wait for my love.

It's at night that I miss Allush the most. Like right now. She and I would lie, holding hands and watching falling stars. We'd whisper until Mollish would shush us. Tell us we should rest. Why didn't I kiss her when I had the chance? I was being so careful not to scare her off. Did she wonder that I didn't? I should have told her I thought we ought to get to know each other better—that I wanted us to start out properly, slowly. That was the only reason I didn't. What if she thinks I didn't want to? What if that's the reason . . . or one of the reasons she went home?

It won't be hard to stay awake. All I have to do is look up at the moon and wish she was next to me. Back then I was too happy to sleep—too excited

being so close to her. Those days were a fog of joy—
of anticipation.

In the morning, here I am, still alive. We start
back, Youpas' hands tied though I don't think they
need to be. He looks as if he doesn't care about anything anymore. But that's a dangerous state, too.
Maybe even more dangerous than rage.

I lead his horse. I'm not going to be much good for
pushing cows while I'm looking after him. Corwin
puts us at the back. Emily drives the truck and trailer
to the next campsite. (We'll have one more day on
the trail.) Then she rides her pony back to help
us, but, for the first half, most of the work is up
to Corwin and Jack. Sore legs, sprained ankle,
wounded face . . . even so, Jack is really helping.

Nobody is having any fun anymore. It's turned
into work. Everybody looks grim. All the horses are
tired and balky even though we're heading home.
They're wondering why they don't have their usual
rest time. Instead they have to carry three big guys
and never get a chance to trade off with a fresh
horse.

WE'RE LATE WHEN WE GET TO THE TRUCK. WE'RE ALL
too tired to eat. Corwin brought energy bars for just
that problem. I notice Jack is too hungry to be picky.
He doesn't even take a bar apart to check on the
nuts and raisins. And he doesn't look soft and pale
anymore. Tired as he is, the way he holds himself,

the way he notices everything, nobody would take him for retarded.

I can see what Emily sees in him. When he took off his shirt and washed in the stream, I saw her staring. Among the natives, only body builders have chests and arms like ours. I still think it odd, though, she'd have to search hard to find a man whose looks were more the opposite from her own. She's being completely unreasonable, but then I am, too. I'm more and more certain that Allush is up at the Secret City waiting for me though I keep telling myself that can't be. Besides, even if she wanted to come back she'd want to see something of her homeworld wouldn't she? If I'd gone back, I'd stay long enough to know what I was rejecting.

Except maybe my people won't let anybody come back anymore. Maybe they want everybody safely home. Maybe they only let the rescuers come. But Allush could put herself on a rescuing team and keep snatching people back until she found me. Then, if she says come home with her, I would because she'd have seen both worlds by then.

That's my daydream—my wishful thinking.

Youpas won't talk to me in the native language nor to Jack in our language though Jack tries to get him to. That's a relief. I don't want them plotting things behind my back.

When Emily rides back to meet us, I see her sizing us up. She's been thinking. She talks to Corwin. Whatever she's trying to convince him of, I can see she fails. He's a down-to-earth kind of person. He won't believe anything as unreasonable as what she might be thinking about us.

Now everybody's angry or upset except Jack. He's as if a child, smiling out at everybody, hoping to change our mood. He's enjoying himself in spite of us and in spite of his sore legs.

A coyote sits in the grass and calmly watches the whole herd of us go by. It's a real beauty—one of those with markings on his face sort of like some malamutes. Jack looks back at me. I nod and make the OK sign and he makes it back at me. My mood does lift as I look at everything as though through his eyes.

We get back to Corwin's late the next day. We three sleep in the barn again. We'll move the cows to the far pasture in the morning and then get paid and leave. Youpas is in such a state I can't tell what he'll do. I don't think he knows himself. He's still not eating though Corwin coaxed him into drinking some coffee. Corwin is like Mollish, good to everybody even though he still thinks Youpas should be arrested.

I don't keep Youpas tied up except at night. I tell him we'll go back. We'll find her. I tell him we'll follow our own tracks back. I say I'm not sure I'll be good at that but he must be, he's the mountain man. I tell him the beacons at the Secret City are the only hope for Jack to go home and for Allush to come back.

Emily goes off to school next morning. She hugs me and Jack. Tells us to come back. "Please, please, *please!*" Jack understands, more or less, that this is good-bye. She says, "Say, I will, Jack. Say, I'll come back." And he says it. Then she tips her cowboy hat low and at an angle, yells, "Ay *Yaa!*" and off she goes. Strides off in her best boots. Too bad, because she was the one made Jack learn fast. But maybe he's still motivated. Maybe he thinks we'll soon be back.

Then the three of us start up into the mountains, me with our useless (and generous) three hundred dollars. Meanwhile my shoes are falling apart, the soles worn through. I've already put cardboard in. I'm jealous of Jack's new boots. My feet will be sopping, not only every time we cross a stream, but even in slightly marshy spots. And it's getting colder. I'll be in real trouble pretty soon.

This first part of the trail is easy. We hike back beyond the wealthy houses, then the road . . . (I'd stop and steal boots, but I don't want to do that yet again and I keep thinking Allush will make me moccasins like hers. I know that's crazy but it pleases me to think it. It even pleases me to be uncomfortable until she makes them for me.) . . . then the dirt road. It's afterwards, from the cliff on—from where I punched Jack—that I'll lose the way. I was watching Allush so intently I didn't pay much attention to anything.

I lead through this first part. Jack limps but he's pretty much OK. Corwin did a good job of binding him up. I found myself a stout stick for a new cane. Youpas lags behind. He doesn't care where we go. He stops to rest any time he feels like it. We keep having to go back for him. He's so depressed I wouldn't be surprised if he doesn't deliberately try to get us all lost. Or lose me and Jack and then go on and get lost by himself. I guess he doesn't think Allush has come back. He's heard her say too often how she wanted to go home.

But now even Jack looks depressed. I never thought he would. But I don't blame him. Not only has he had to say good-bye to Emily, but here he is hiking back into the mountains, sleeping on the ground again. I try to tell him about the Secret City. I'd ask Youpas to do it, but I don't like them talking to each other when I can't tell what they're saying. Not that Youpas would perk up enough to do it anyway.

Jack is still asking the names of things and practicing the words he knows. Some actual phrases. "That up in there is blue. This down in here is all green and there is green, too. What is that color over there? Rainbow. Rainbow. Wow! Where water is it? Outta sight. We have it. Betasha."

We camp that first night just beyond the houses in the same spot Jack and I did, hidden in the trees a few yards from the stream. I tie up Youpas' hands. He doesn't care.

I wake up smelling coffee and bacon. We hadn't brought any bacon and no real coffee, only instant.

There's a whinny and the thumping of a hobbled horse. At first I think I'm back with Corwin, bringing down the cows. Then I wake up enough to know that can't be. I struggle out of my sleeping bag. Trying to hurry makes it all the slower.

And here, yet again and more of a surprise than ever, is Emily.

I force myself to slow down, put on my pants and shoes. I walk over and squat down beside her. I accept a cup. I sit and sip. I feel just as resigned and silent as her father was. How get out of this mess? What to say? Thanks for the bacon? Thanks for breakfast?

I say, "Does your father know you're here?"

"Of course not. Well, maybe by now. At least he knows I'm somewhere I'm not supposed to be."

She caught up with us easily because she has her pony. She actually went through a whole day of school before following us. She's still in her school clothes, that flowery blouse and jeans. Jack already made a fuss about that blouse. She actually has her homework with her. It's on the ground beside her. She must have been working on it before she made breakfast.

Jack can't stop smiling. Youpas is horrified. I'm worried. I told Corwin I could keep things in line, but now I'm not so sure I can.

Youpas leans close to me and says, "We have to get rid of her. We can't go anywhere near the Secret City with one of *them*."

He's right of course, but I decide I'll just sit down and enjoy this next half hour, bacon and decent coffee. There's nothing else to do.

ALLUSH

I CAN'T BELIEVE HERE I AM, NOT ONLY LOOKING FOR two lost . . . I mean now just one lost man and Lorpas . . . but also looking for Youpas. He's a wealthy man. Definitely one of the "right kind." I can't imagine our Secret City butcher owning one of those towers. If he's the right kind I'm not eager to be it.

I wonder if Mollish could have been my real mother? I've heard that our people handed babies around like that more than most natives here do, though they say the Chinese used to do it. Mollish did treat me as her child but I sure didn't treat her as my mother. Actually I didn't treat my mother as my mother either. But that Mollish is my real mother is the only reason I can think that they wouldn't know what kind I was. Is that another reason I shouldn't go back to our world?

But there's another reason that Youpas should go

back. Here, he's killed three archeologists. If they ever find out who did it, he'll be WANTED.

But wouldn't that be nice . . . to have Mollish as your mother? I look like her, too.

I feel worse again—that I can't talk to her about it. I wrap the scarf close around my neck and shoulders. I tell it I'm sorry—sorry, sorry.

But I don't think I'll ever figure out why I'm not the right kind. I've thought and thought about how the people looked there. Back at that fancy dinner, everybody looked the same, the waiters, the dancers, and yet everybody seemed to know about me right away. Did Olowpas dress me some special way? Wrong kind of clothes? Or did he make some gestures I didn't understand?

Will they look at Youpas and know right away that he's the right kind?

The waiter stepped on my toe surreptitiously. Spilled things on me. Well, only water. Probably ruined that blouse, but I'm not one to care much about clothes. Sitting right there, listening to that screeching, I was wishing I was back here and up in one of my trees.

But I don't want to be any kind of a kind. How come our parents never said a word about it? They must have been ashamed that there was an underclass. Maybe nobody *ever* talked about it. But why didn't Mollish tell me? She wasn't afraid to say anything. I think she was the wrong kind, but up there in the Secret City she got to be the most important one of all of us. Her death is the worst thing. Lorpas thought she was the last of the old ones. Maybe she didn't tell me about untouchables because I was one, too, and she didn't want me to feel bad, but I wouldn't have cared. I didn't even care if I was the wrong kind when I was there.

My parents didn't know how to do anything for themselves. All they did was take notes on this world so that when they got back they could give programs about it. But the way we lived—they were hardly really on this world at all—isolated up there because this world wasn't good enough for us. I wonder what they thought they were taking notes on. Maybe just flora and fauna. Though I was the one knew all about those.

How I'm dressed now... will I look all right for the Down? For sure not my hair. Mollish's green scarf is nice and warm and wooly, but is a handknit scarf civilized enough? And this weird suit. The shoes are part of the pants. I'd need a pair of scissors to get rid of the shoes and keep the pants. The pants have pockets all down the sides just like Olowpas' pants did, so they make me look bowlegged. They seemed to like that look back there, but I hope Lorpas never sees me in them.

Lorpas said, as long as we went east, there was no way we wouldn't end up on the main road. He told about which town he had to avoid because he'd been in jail there, so at least I know where he isn't. He told about how nice the old woman he lived with was even though she was a native. He was trying to get me to like it here, but I wonder if I could have stayed if I'd tried. They were so fast. Besides, that's how Lorpas got burned. If I'd fought they might have burned me, too. I wonder how he is. I don't think he's dead, though. Wouldn't his body be there at the cliff if he was?

Before I start in any direction at all, I should wash my hair. For sure Lorpas will never recognize me with my hair this short and might not even with the stiffener and the curls and the black are washed out. How am I going to prove I'm me?

But I don't start. I sit the way I did when I was next to Mollish—to her bones that is. Only when I remind myself that I have her scarf right here, around my neck, do I think: she's really dead.

I notice things more than usual. There's still a lot of little creatures around. Junkos, jays. . . . Something keeps squawking. That's exactly how I feel. I imitate it. It doesn't help. I stop and just stare. The aspen rustle. Right in front of me there are leaves more golden than gold. I pick up a dead pennyroyal seed-head, crush it and hold it to my nose. I rub it on my hands. Then I decide. Nobody wants to be up there in the Secret City in the winter. Even Mollish didn't want to spend another winter up there. All the more reason not to go there. If I don't look too odd dressed like this I'll go down.

Why, *why* didn't our parents let us grow up with the natives! I hardly know anything about either world. And if my parents had lived in the Down with the natives, we'd have had telephone numbers. Maybe Lorpas has a telephone number.

But I can't sit here and feel bad all day. I'm going Down.

◡   ◡   ◡

LORPAS

I WATCH JACK WATCHING EMILY. I WATCH HER watching him. Is it a rule that people have to fall in love with the most unsuitable mate? Except I didn't. I fell in love with the very first suitable woman I met. I fell for Allush because she was my kind. Of course Jack and I grew up completely the opposite, I, surrounded by natives, and Jack, surrounded by only us. I guess it makes sense, the most rare is always the most attractive.

But Emily *is* something special—of any kind of person, theirs or ours. Looks like a pale little waif but she's a tough and competent motherless child. She has that special smile, lips working, as if she thinks she shouldn't smile. There's that shy duck of her head. No wonder Jack is so taken. I wonder, though, does he really appreciate her as I do and as one of her own kind would? Or is she just intriguingly odd to him?

Whatever happens . . . and it better not . . . I'll not let any harm come to her. Besides, I told Corwin I'd take care of things. He trusts me and I promised. He'd have gone to the police if I hadn't.

But, for sure, if Emily is here, Corwin will be right behind. It won't be hard for him to guess where she's gone. And for sure, Emily knows he'll follow. For all I know, she left clues all along the trail just to make sure he would. She knows she can count on him for anything and everything.

Emily wants to talk to me privately. Everybody seems to think I'm in charge. Ever since I was halfway grown-up they always did. Even Mother. Soon as Father died, I was the boss. That is, the boss of everything except for the decision about going home. The rule was, that she should go when they came for us and that I should go back with her whether I wanted to or not.

Emily and I hike back down the river trail to a pleasant sitting spot. You can hardly tell the sounds of blowing cottonwood leaves from the sound of the stream. Everything rustling. And on top of that, the sounds of birds. Mostly raucous jays. Emily sits with her feet hanging over the grassy bank, almost in the water, and I sit on a rock.

I'm worried though, about leaving Jack and

Youpas by themselves. What are they going to think up? Of course I'd never know anyway, whether I was there or not.

I say, "You know and I know, your father's right behind you."

She ignores me and starts right off with, "Who are you guys? You're not like us. And you're not brothers. And your names—I heard you—Jack isn't even named Jack. You know what you look like to me? Neanderthals. We studied all about you. Did your people hide out someplace and keep on existing? Did you even keep your secret Neanderthal language? I never heard of a language with sniffs. Except you don't know how to speak it, do you, but Jack does and so does that other one."

Better that than the reality. I'll say, You guessed it. But before I can, she says, "But that's not what I really, really, really think. I think you came from some other planet."

There it is.

Is she planning to save the world? From us? But it's us who are afraid of her kind and always have been.

If we really are from a world where some kind of Neanderthal types survived . . . not so dumb, by the way . . . then, if the natives take us over, it won't be the first time some dexterous, fine boned version of Homo sapiens sapiens has wiped us out.

What are we supposed to do when a native discovers what we are? We haven't faced that problem, at least that I know of. Or at least they never told me. Maybe they never told me because what they did was too vicious to contemplate. Would my people do that? And after all their talk about being better—kinder—than the natives? And who was in charge of taking care of that . . . that disposal? And what if said knowledgeable Homo sapiens sapiens is Emily? Take her along? Show her the Secret City?

I won't let any harm come to her if my life depends on it. First Ruth and then this girl. I've seldom felt as close to natives as I have with these two. And Corwin, also. The good father.

But Emily says she did the opposite of leaving a trail. She says, "My dad can't follow. I laid a trail off to the side. At least it'll take him a long time to get back on track. Where are you going, anyway? There's nothing way out here and it's getting cold."

"It is."

Best not to confess anything—yet. If ever. Thank goodness she's a kid and nobody will believe her. "Do you have your sleeping bag?"

"'Course. And you know what? I don't believe Jack is dumb. He's just as smart as anybody. Maybe smarter. Look how fast he learns things. But, and you know what? He's never even used a spoon and fork before. He's never even eaten peas. He didn't know what they were. And he ate the whole apple, stem and seeds and all. And how can you not like chocolate?"

"Emily, can you just keep quiet about this for awhile? Maybe not talk about it even with Corwin?"

"Maybe."

"Please. Just for now."

"Maybe."

BUT I'VE FORGOTTEN ALL ABOUT YOUPAS AND JACK. On the way back up the path, I suddenly get suspicious. I tell Emily to stay behind me and keep quiet while I creep up on our campsite.

I come upon them whispering furiously together. Looks like Jack is taking my side. But then Youpas grabs a firebrand. I rush in just as he swings it at Jack.

There it is again. I'm getting tired of always being, not only the one in charge, but the main target. Though, well, Jack has that scratch across his cheek and a not-so-good ankle. But Youpas doesn't have a mark on him that I know of. I'd like to change that.

I sit on Youpas' legs, catch my breath, and check on the burned arm of my jacket. That old corduroy jacket is looking worse than ever.

Nobody says a word.

Jack has found the piece of rope we've been tying Youpas with. Emily stands by looking worried, but not for long. Here she is, already back from the stream, with a cold wet cloth for my burns but I don't have any.

I wave her away.

And now, just as I figured but sooner than I thought—sooner than Emily thought, too—here's Corwin. He rides up on his little blue roan. Quiet, not even a Hello to anybody. Always quiet when he's angry or upset.

Youpas, tied and hobbled, but still the butcher, says, "She knows, doesn't she. You know what to do, and if you can't do it, I can."

I'm sure Corwin is about to say the same thing about Youpas though not quite as drastic as what Youpas wants for Emily. Just the police. I can see it on Corwin's face as he looks at me. An: I told you so, sort of look, and: I was afraid you couldn't keep him out of trouble.

I wish, more than ever, for Mollish and her wisdom—especially her knowledge of both worlds. Neanderthals indeed! Not paying attention when knowledge walked right beside you! Is that why they were wiped out on this world? Or because they were like Mother, wanting their own, old ways and no others?

Of course the fact that we look like this world's Neanderthals has nothing to do with anything. Only that we come from a colder, harsher world.

Corwin takes Emily off for a private talking to while I start packing up. Jack helps. By now he knows how as well as I do.

When they come back Emily won't look at any of us. Corwin hardly will either. He says, "So. . . .

So. . . . We'll be heading back and you'll be keeping on . . . like you promised."

I try to say I'm sorry, but he says, "It's not your fault." Then he says, "She has a cockamamie story."

"I know."

"But why. . . . Why in the world *are* you heading up into the mountains in this season? One thing at least, she's right about Jack. I sure don't believe your story about him being feebleminded. Where did he come from?"

He looks over at Jack and Youpas. Jack packing up and Youpas glowering. He stares. Then stares back at me. I can see understanding coming to his face.

"It's not a cockamamie story is it?"

I don't want to kill anybody, least of all my friends. Actually I don't even want to kill Youpas. It hasn't been easy, but I've managed to get along so far, even in prison without killing anybody. And would it be so terrible if natives like Corwin and Emily knew where we came from?

Besides, I know about his hidden pistol and so does Youpas.

I tell him right out. "I'm supposed to get rid of you before you reveal us, but I'm not going to do it."

An ironic, "Thanks a lot." And then a more friendly, "I know you won't."

It's then Corwin looks down at my shoes, and back up at me. "You're in trouble already."

"I know."

He goes to his pack and pulls out a pair of wool socks. "You're going to need these more than I will. What's up there in the mountains anyway? Some sort of spaceship or flying saucer?"

I don't say. Let him go on and think what he needs to think. Better a flying saucer than a Secret City, or at least no worse. I do tell him we're not sure of the way back. I say, "You . . . Hugh . . . " (Hugh!) ". . . might prefer we all freeze to death. Best you and Emily leave us before we get too lost to ever get anywhere at all."

Corwin tells Emily she already said enough good-byes yesterday for several more going-aways and she should come now. *Now*!

He gives me a friendly punch on the shoulder. (I feel privileged that he does.) And they mount up.

Jack watches as they leave, then sits down dejected. I feel just as bad. Socks are not going to help much with shoes as worn-out as mine. And why did I ever think Allush could be back at the Secret City waiting for me?

Youpas, still tied and flat out on the ground, frowns up at me, says, "If this whole thing is discovered you'll be the first on my list to go and they'll be second."

I say, "I was already first on that list of yours a long time ago."

We load up and start out when Jack suddenly stops, sits down and yells, "Ayy *yaa*. No! I no good-bye. I no go. I no! I no!"

Youpas sits down beside him and smiles a "so there" smile up at me.

Mutiny. On both sides. I'm not surprised or even sorry. It'll be against my promise to Corwin but we can leave later. Our three hundred dollars would buy me shoes and us a night or two in town and a couple of good meals. We all need a rest.

I'll have to make sure Jack doesn't get back to Corwin's. It still worries me though, that Jack has no idea that Emily is just a kid. Maybe a little more time in town would help him see that. Maybe if we people-watch in the park again. Maybe that would give him the right idea.

But what to do with Youpas . . . still dressed as a mountain man, unshaven, hair a filthy mop? Maybe Jack and I together. . . .

We do it. It's not hard. Youpas' hands are still tied and I'm the one with the know-how for fighting. Again, just as Jack thought when I washed the dye and stiffener out of his hair, Youpas thinks we're trying to drown him. He's relieved when he finds out it isn't so. In fact, just like Jack felt, he looks downright grateful not to end up drowned.

I hate to steal from that same summer house yet again but that was the house with clothes for a big man. I break in again. Same window. We pull and push each other up and through it. I find scissors and cut Youpas' hair and all of his beard off. I boil up some warm water on that camping stove and shave him. At first Jack holds him down but he isn't struggling anymore, though he could be waiting for his chance.

Afterwards he's a whole new man. He's younger than I thought, too. Both he and Jack are probably hardly mid-twenties in this world's calculation. For some reason that makes me feel more sympathetic to him. Killing the beautiful white mule. . . . That was the desperation of the young in love.

Looks like he hardly recognizes himself. He studies himself in the three-way mirror in the big bedroom, turning side to side. Looks like he likes what he sees. Can't get enough. I leave him admiring himself and find some worn out hiking boots. Jack already got the new ones from this house. Besides, where stealing is concerned, enough's enough.

We've all taken showers. Cold ones. Youpas picks out a shirt, a sweater, and a pair of pants to his liking. Striped cowboy shirt and fancy black leather vest. I don't stop him. Puts them on and studies himself again. That first time we were here, I had a hard time getting Jack out of the big bed. This time it looks like I'll have a hard time getting Youpas away from the mirror.

(This time Jack eats the spaghetti, no problem.)

I'm tempted to leave our three hundred dollars in a conspicuous place to pay for what we've taken and the broken window, but I don't know what we'd do without it.

And then I steal yet another thing—I promise myself I'll come back someday and leave money—I take that silky skirt I saw in the closet last time I was here. It's light, it rolls into a ball no bigger than a pair of socks. I may never see Allush again, but I take it for her.

So, with the day half gone, we head back to town. Youpas has changed. I seem, now, to have two of them looking up to me as though I know what to do next. They're both willing to do what I say. Couldn't just be the clothes and haircut, could it? Youpas all slicked up and admiring himself? Wanting to act like a real human being? Like Homo sapiens sapiens? Or should I say, a real Neanderthal?

Maybe now I can get him to tell Jack to lay off Emily, that she's not a prime example of native womanhood, but a prime example of a child. Though for all I know Youpas will tell him, Go ahead, and, good luck.

We spend the night in cabins. I sign in with an old address my parents had when we lived just outside of L.A. The cabins are the old-fashioned kind—separated from each other. Not very good beds. The pictures on the walls are cut out of magazines—flowers or cute children. There's a little kitchen. (A big sign over the sink says: Don't Clean Fish Here!!! Three exclamation points.) I show Jack and Youpas how to work the stove. I fill up the ice trays. Even Youpas hasn't seen any of these things since he was a kid. He starts Jack saying, "Oh boy, oh boy," and Jack gets Youpas to saying, "Outta sight."

The corner store is in walking distance (actually

everything is) and we get an assortment of groceries. Lots of fruit. That's what Jack has least trouble eating.

Youpas looks around at everything just as much as Jack does. They window-shop. It takes a long time to get to the store and back. As we pass the park, I buy them ice-cream cones at the little stand there and we sit on a bench to eat them.

Jack says, "Cold, too much," and I say, "That's OK. It's supposed to be."

I ask Youpas how old he was when he went up to the Secret City and he says, "Six."

"Did you want to go?"

"Of course not." He practically yells it. "I missed all the things we had down here. Like this ice cream. I had friends and lots of toys. My parents made me give away all my toys but one."

"What toy did you keep?"

"It had to be something small. A little truck. A red one that dumped. I lost it up there. My fire engine was too big to bring. I told my parents I wanted to grow up to be a fireman. They said I was too important to be a fireman. After a while I practically forgot what trucks were."

"If my parents had known about the city, I'd have been up there with you."

"They said the city was a waiting place—just for a little while and we'd go home, but after a couple of years of it even our parents got bored and started building the Secret City—for something to do. They were also trying to show us kids how marvelous it was back home but I think they mostly did it because they were just as bored as we kids were. Everybody was unhappy. Maybe not Allush. She was climbing trees and taming animals the minute we got there. It's funny that she wanted to go home so much."

"How about you? You want to go home?"

"I don't know. My parents said I'd be important back there so maybe."

Later, when we're in front of a hardware store window, I'm feeling sorry for him. I say, "We could spare some money. Is there something you want?"

He gives me a look. He's thinking about me, not about what he might want me to buy. He's trusting me. Maybe even liking me. Then he says, "I'll think about it." Then he thinks again, says, "You want to go back to the city because of Allush don't you."

"I don't know where else to go that she could find me."

"Winter was no fun up there. We were holed up like moles." Then, "*Rats*!" he says. "More like rats. I hated it."

"Back at the city, Jack can get homing devices and go home if he wants to. Does he want to?"

"He's pretty fascinated with everything here right now, and there's that girl."

"She's only thirteen for heaven's sake. Tell him."

They talk. Then Youpas says. "He doesn't believe me. He says she cares about him, too. He says she followed us because of him."

Youpas says I should do something about Emily and Corwin. They know about us. "All the more dangerous, if Emily's a kid, she'll tell somebody."

"Nobody will believe a kid."

"For all we know she has proof. Or maybe she knows how to get proof."

"Why would she want to tell on us? She likes Jack." I raise my hands up and out on both sides. "I don't know what to do."

Youpas laughs. "That's a gesture our parents always made. You're still one of us."

Makes me realize I haven't heard him laugh before. He seems so changed. Could getting out of that place, getting all cleaned up, being down here with everything new . . . could these, just like that, have tipped him over into sanity? Made him realize there's a big world out here? Except he still wants to kill people.

I had thought to buy him a nice hunter's knife that would fit on his belt and then I think: Maybe not, considering.

BACK AT THE MOTEL, GETTING READY FOR BED, JACK and I start to tie up Youpas again, but he says, "Trust me. Please. We want the same things and we can help each other."

Then he says it over again in the home language for Jack. Or it seems he does. As usual I can make out words such as: "and" and "but" and "also," but nothing important.

He looks such a different person lying there—waiting to be tied. Even has his wrists held out. He's all slicked up. Handsome . . . our kind of handsome. What will Allush think when she sees him?

I say, "Maybe." But Jack says, "OK, OK."

So I guess that's it.

They share a bed and I get to sleep by myself. They defer to me. Again as if I'm in charge.

They both fall right to sleep, happy to be in a bed for a change, but my mind goes on and on. I wonder about Allush appearing back on this world looking for me. What if she comes to the Down in a hairdo like Jack's? In ridiculous clothes all wrong for the weather? Would I recognize her? I wouldn't, anymore than I would have recognized Youpas.

And there's that skirt I stole. I should feel guilty—and I do—but I also can't wait to give it to her. It's so wonderfully soft and flimsy. Of course it's the wrong season for such a light material. But maybe she doesn't like skirts. She seems like a tomboy. Except she had to be, living up there in the wilds, there was no other way.

And someday I'd like to get hiking boots for her, that is if she wants to go back to the Secret City.

I'd like to get her a ring though our people seldom wear them. Our knuckles are too big. She might wear one, though, if I asked her to.

And I want to bring back another white mule. I

know it can't ever be as magical and mysterious as the other one. You can't ever replace an old love with something that looks like your love but isn't. Maybe a mule-colored mule would be best so as not to remind Allush of what happened.

It wouldn't be just for Allush, but for us, too. It would help us get back to the city. He ... she ... could carry our packs and we could ride her now and then.

But I'm fooling myself. The homeworld is what she always wanted. Is she there right now enjoying herself? Meeting new people. New men. I wonder if she'd try to come back for my sake.

I look at the clock. Three twenty-five. I'm wasting this nice bed. I wish I had some kind of pill or other.

I WAKE UP LATE, STILL TIRED. IT'S ALMOST ELEVEN. I don't want to get out of bed and I'm hoping Jack and Youpas don't want to either.

I look at the other bed. But they're gone. I jump up—scared. I'm thinking they're off at Corwin's to kidnap Emily—and she'd be glad to go with them. Or to kill people, or maybe they're off to L.A. Youpas spoke of wanting to go there. Jack knows how to hitchhike. My God, both of them babes in the woods. I'll never find them.

And they took my wallet with our money. Now I'm sure they're gone. Well, half of it belongs to Jack so I guess that's fair.

I throw on my clothes and rush out.

And there they are, cross-legged on a grassy spot in front of the motel, gabbing away in our home language. They've got hamburgers and drinks from McDonald's. Jack is eating with as much gusto as Youpas. Youpas hands me a cup of coffee and my wallet. I collapse down beside them. It's a little while before I can eat or drink.

INSTEAD OF A WHITE MULE, I SETTLE FOR A BURRO. She's beautiful in a different way from the mule: Black ears, mane, and tail, white underbelly, gray back, white nose. Dignified and gentle. A down-to-earth creature. Not at all magical.

She was free at the donkey rescue center. All you have to do is give a donation and bring her back a month later so they can check to see that she's well cared for. I say, I will, but, if they don't mind, maybe a little late. I'm taking her into the mountains.

I let her stay in a field just outside of town temporarily, which is where she was in the first place. I'll pick her up when we're on our way. She'll be sad, leaving her donkey friends. I wonder if I should rescue two of them so she'll have company.

Her name is Toots. It doesn't fit her. She's too serious and quiet.

But I'm not so sure we're going anywhere anytime soon. Jack doesn't want to start camping again and he doesn't want to leave the town were Emily lives, and Youpas wants to stay here, too, maybe to kill the person Jack's in love with and her father. Allush said he's already killed three people. She said he'd have no qualms about killing natives. All he knows about the Down he read in books. I should try to explain that here in civilization, he won't get away with it. And once they arrest him, our people could be in trouble.

When I speak to Youpas about it he says, "This land is getting all used up fast. One of these days they'll have to raid some other world. This world can't last as it is."

"Corwin and Emily won't tell."

"I know these people."

"How can you? You've been up there since you were a little kid. All you know is what our old ones told you. And with you in prison for murder the natives may find out about us all the faster. And I don't know why you're so worried. We're the only ones that have the means to get them on our world. Unlikely they'll ever discover how we do it. And, by the way, I'll defend Corwin and Emily with my life. You know I will."

"And I'm willing to risk *my* life for the sake of our world."

"If they find you or me dead you're risking our world, too."

"Not as much. Maybe not at all. Besides, they're not going to find *you*. I can see to that."

"Maybe."

"You're still first on my list."
"I thought we were friends now."

○   ○   ○

ALLUSH

FIRST THING, I FALL. I WAS TAKING RISKS LIKE I always do, but now that I'm alone in the middle of the mountains, I shouldn't. Mollish said over and over that I should be more careful. She said she didn't want to find me lying under a tree with a broken leg.

I was striding along yet another rocky narrow spot. I fall flat, hit my chin hard and rip the pants of this special suit. It was already badly torn from sliding down the scree. It may keep me dry and warm, but it's nothing like my old dearskin clothes for comfort and strength. I thought everything back home was supposed to be better and more advanced than anything here on this world, and those old clothes were just old-fashioned leather but they were the best. Now my bloody knees are hanging out. What will happen if I fall on my fanny? Not unusual when going down steep hills. I'll be bare both front and back. At least my homeworld believes in underwear.

Good thing I fell, though. Now I'll be more careful.

It'll be warmer in the Down, but I'm never going to take off this scarf. Never. I don't care how hot it gets. I saw Mollish knitting away at it. Must have been a couple of winters ago. She knit one for me first. I wonder where it got to. I probably left it in the top of tree when I was too hot one day. I didn't care about anything. I thought: She'll just knit me another one.

I can't eat that home food. I have to find something else and fast. They did give me a knife, so sharp it'll shave the hair off your arm. (That's how Youpas tested his knives for butchering.) A good knife was all I asked for. I was always proud to be able to get along in the wilds. I hardly ever went home at lunchtime. Me and my fox—we mostly ate in the woods where we could eat together and not be bothered by other people—people that disapproved of both of us. Not counting Mollish, though.

I never did find out if there are any wild spots on the home world. I should have asked if it was nothing but towers. I wouldn't like that at all.

This time of year the animals are in the warmer valleys—what few that aren't huddled up for the winter. I hate to waste time on food, but I just can't abide that goo of theirs.

I can't catch a fish by hand like Lorpas did—I tried and I never managed it. I make a little trip-trap. Fifteen minutes later I have a quail. I move the trap and set it again, then I use the stikers from the home world to light a fire. While the first one is cooking I catch two more. They're small, but I'll have enough now for a day or two. I'll be hungry but I won't starve.

Needless to say, I don't get far this day either. At this rate I'll never get anywhere. First the storm, then finding Mollish and then sitting for half a day and hardly knowing I'm doing it. Mollish would have said moping, but it wasn't moping this time. I needed time to realize she wasn't here anymore. I needed time to think about how much I loved her.

I find a big tree that fell, its torn out roots form a wall of earth. On the clean side where the trunk is, there's a nice sheltered spot. I wrap up my quail tight and hang them from a branch several yards away and then crawl under the tree trunk. Tomorrow I'll hurry. I'll eat on the run, but I'll be careful, too.

LORPAS

THEY'VE BEEN TALKING IT OVER. ALL OF A SUDDEN I'm not in charge of anything anymore.

They've been wandering around town from the

baseball diamond all the way to the fish hatchery, me, trailing after. Now and then I get to explain a thing or two but mostly they talk our home language. I've no idea what about.

It's a small town, just a little cluster of stores along Main Street. One store is nothing but fishing poles and rifles. There's one grocery store, one gas station—more motels than anything else and most of those are old, and mostly empty this time of year. The library is in a normal house. So is the Paiute museum. The high school and the elementary school are two blocks back from Main Street. They share the same playing field.

Jack and Youpas walk past the schools several times. I suppose looking for Emily. They stand for awhile and watch a soccer game. Girls playing, but thank goodness not Emily. These girls are a little younger. Is Jack getting any idea, now, of ages?

I try, again, to tell him. "These are children. Child. Children. Babies." I gesture sizes. I say, "Emily. A child."

Jack just looks at me.

"Youpas, tell him."

"You can't ever tell people what they don't want to know."

JACK HAS DECIDED HE LIKES ICE CREAM AS LONG AS it doesn't have anything lumpy in it like nuts and they both like McDonald's. At least we're not spending a lot of money on food, though I have a yearning to take them both to a nice restaurant with waiters or waitresses. It might have a good effect, especially on Youpas.

That evening they go to a local baseball game and shout themselves hoarse along with the natives, though they have no idea how the game is played. I try to explain it to them, but they don't want to know. I think again how young they are. And one a complete savage and the other utterly ignorant of this world. Actually they're equally ignorant but in different ways.

Allush. . . . She's a savage, too. I wonder. . . . Maybe she thinks more or less as Youpas does about the natives. That's what the old ones taught us. Except I don't think Mollish felt that way.

WE SPEND ANOTHER NIGHT AT THE MOTEL. I COUNT out what's left of the money and show them. Not enough for much more than one cheap meal and a few more supplies for the trip.

Jack says, "One, two, three, four, five, no good."

"We can't stay. Are you ready to go? There's nothing else to do."

I *hope* there's nothing else to do. Who knows what they'll conjure up.

They discuss it with each other—again, in the home language—but not with me. Finally Jack says, "OK, OK." And we pack up.

I wonder if they actually are going to leave.

I check for my knife. I still have it.

We head for the outskirts of town, west toward the mountains. My donkey is in a field not far beyond the schools. We have to pass the schools first.

But here's Emily, waiting on the front steps of the high school as if expecting us. She's leaning against the door in a kind of teenager's slouch, her black cowboy hat pulled low over her eyes as usual. I almost expect a cigarette drooping in her mouth, except I know she's against them. As soon as she sees us, she rushes up to Jack. Now looking more like a little kid than a teenager. Hugs him. Yells, "I knew you'd come."

She has a bigger backpack than her usual school bag. She's ready to go.

How did they ever get word to her without me knowing? Have they mastered the telephone, and quarters, and the telephone book without my help?

"And now," Youpas says, mostly to me, "We're headed for Los Angeles."

I should have guessed. That's where all three want to go.

"With no money? And there's too many of us to hitchhike."

Youpas says, "*You* won't be with us," while Jack says, "Truck. Truckses."

Is Jack, against me, too? Even Jack?

Look how they stand, relaxed, Jack's arm across Emily's shoulder, Youpas, hands on hips.

Youpas says, "First there's Corwin."

"In front of Emily!"

"First after we deal with you."

Look how they stand. A couple of innocents.

"You're the one, going to get our people discovered. If you kill somebody, the natives will find you in a minute, and I don't want Jack getting into this kind of trouble before he hardly knows where he is."

"I killed before. Up at the city. The old ones told me to. We have to save our homeworld."

"Up there in the mountains it's a little different. Though I can promise you these natives are still looking for the bodies *and* the murderer."

"All the more reason. . . . I've nothing to lose. Besides, we're smarter than they are. They'll never catch one of *us*."

"Hah."

"We wouldn't be here if we weren't smarter. Instead they'd be on our world."

Except. . . .

Not a problem.

Not yet anyway.

Youpas still stands, hands on hips. Jack is looking down at Emily. A couple of innocents.

Only question is who gets which?

Fast! One uppercut, twist, then one kick. Two down right in front of the school. Well, at least behind the trees and bushes that line the front walkway.

I'm in charge again.

I think.

Emily just stands there. The look on her face doesn't match the jaunty angle of her hat.

Youpas is still groggy. I hit him hard. I turn and help Jack up.

I have no idea whose side Jack is on, though maybe Youpas has given him a crazy idea of this world. Could he have convinced Jack that killing is necessary to save our planet?

Youpas is really knocked out. I splash his face with water from my canteen. Then I help him up, too, but I hang on to his arm, twisted up behind him, good and tight.

Just when I thought he was a changed man.

"Look at yourself. Look how you're dressed. You're not the butcher anymore. You're down here in civilization. You can have a completely new kind of life here."

Do I mean even if he's already a murderer? Even if he killed their mule? Do I think my words will change his mind about anything? And what in the world is he going to do with Emily?

Jack just looks at me. "Whose side are you on, anyway, Jack?"

"Anyway? Anyway?"

The tune is off for a question in English, but I recognize it from the tunes of my parents' speech. *Big* question. He hasn't used that tune before. Except I don't know what he's asking.

And I don't know if Emily is safe from Youpas, or safe from Jack either, in a different way.

But I have, suddenly, such yearning. Not only for Allush, but to be rid of all these people. To be alone and climbing the mountains by myself as I did before. To be heading toward Allush and that she would drop from a tree as she did before and then that there'd be just the two of us. But it's more likely I'll never see her again.

YET AGAIN, WE TIE UP YOUPAS.

I stop and pick up the burro. Load her up. I wonder if she's safe with Youpas around.

I tell Jack I'm going after Allush. I don't tell him I'm going even though I don't believe she's there. "Do as you please. Stay or come."

Jack says, "I do come."

"Emily, I think you should go home."

"I'm going with Jack."

"Corwin will be right behind you."

"Not this time. He thinks I'm staying with a friend. That's not a lie, I *am* staying with a friend."

"Emily, this is all wrong and you know it. You're a kid, for heaven's sake."

"I never liked anybody in the whole wide world as much as I like Jack. And I'm mature for my age. Lots of people say so."

"Running off with Jack at thirteen doesn't seem that mature to me."

"I've heard all this before. Dad already talked to me a *hundred* times. I don't need everybody doing it all over again."

"It hasn't sunk in. Besides, Corwin will blame me if he sees Jack around you. He'll be angry enough to shoot me *and* Jack."

"Then I'll jump in front of Jack so he won't get shot."

"You've been watching too much TV."

What have I got myself into with all these children?

Am I trying to save Youpas by getting him up to the Secret City? What will I do with him up there? Besides, he'll go back to being wild. But he's still wild even down here, haircut, nice clothes, and all.

Off we go again. Maybe.

CORWIN HAS EIGHTY ACRES ON THIS SIDE OF TOWN. Emily wants us to take a back way, a dirt road that winds around the edges of his property. I want to stay on the main road even though we'll pass nearer to Corwin's house. I don't want to circle round and round, maybe add an extra hour. I want to get away from town as fast as possible. But what's the hurry? What does it matter? I give up. I hardly know what I'm doing or why.

I stroke Toots. I've just loaded her up with most of our stuff, but she nuzzles into my chest anyway.

We're already friends. At least there's one dependable creature here. I hope I can keep her safe.

"All right, all right, we'll go your way, but who's to say Corwin won't be out there riding his fences?"

We turn away from the main road and start along the little dirt one that circles Corwin's fields. Maybe just as well, less traffic and fewer people to notice the crazies heading up into the cold. Better on Toots' feet, too, though as soon as we pass the summer people's houses the road will turn to dirt, anyway.

I turn around to see how my troop is coming along and I see there's someone coming down the main road with the loose stride of a mountaineer, big pack as high as his head. He's dressed in a jumpsuit. All sorts of things are hanging on his belt. His legs look funny. Or there's something odd about the pants. He's fallen, the knees of his pants are torn, also his elbows. Around his neck there's a green scarf so frayed I can see strands of yarn hanging from it even from here. I've seen that scarf before. I've joked about it. But Mollish is dead. Whoever has that scarf has got to have slid down all that scree to her body and taken it right from her neck.

But it's a woman. Hair as short as a man's. She's turning. She's starting to run towards us.

Even as I'm thinking: Who? I'm thinking: But I don't recognize her, and then I think: *Yes*! And I run.

She comes straight to me, hugs me, crying. Big breaths—panting as if she can't breath. I. . . . I'm all she wanted. All she wants. But I'm crying, too.

We hold each other. I kiss her . . . at last kiss, really kiss, a long, long kiss, and she kisses me back. It's as if we want to engulf each other with our kisses. Hold each other prisoner forever with our kisses and our hug. Then I kiss her tears. She isn't going to let go of me. We fall on our knees, still holding each other.

I've never had a woman in my arms before. Never. Not to hold close and kiss. I've been a loner for so long. Never even hoped. After all, I'm a bum. Allush is holding on to me as if I'm her hope, her savior. I will be. All else falls away. It's settled. No need to talk about it. No need to ask. *The* question. She looks up at me—the face of my own people . . . a finer version of my own. In my arms . . . warm . . . warm cheeks. . . .

I forget all about Youpas.

Then I hear Emily shout, "He's loose."

I see him trotting away, already a couple of hundred yards down the road towards Corwin's house.

I don't care. Again, and even more so, I want to be done with all this and all these people. I want to give Allush the skirt I stole for her and I want for us to go off alone together. I don't want to stop kissing her—holding her.

Except I have to care.

"Jack, did you?"

I hope he didn't.

"OK."

For once he says it only once.

Allush won't let go, but I tear myself from her arms and take off after Youpas.

I'm wondering if Corwin has his pistol handy. I wonder, is Jack on Youpas' side now for the sake of our people? Will he try to convince Allush to join them? But surely Allush didn't recognize Youpas. I wouldn't have myself if I hadn't been there for the transformation. I wouldn't have recognized Allush if I hadn't seen it happen with Youpas. But, yes, I would. I knew. My body knew. I could feel that it was her.

ALLUSH

WE HUG AND KISS AS IF WE'D ALREADY BEEN LOVERS and couldn't wait to make love again. Our first kisses were so hard and insistent. So grasping. Both of us. He holds me too tight, I can hardly breathe. But I can't breathe right now anyway.

Then he's pushing me away.

"Lorpas!"

"I have to. Wait for me."

"No!"

I throw down my pack and start after him. But the man, one of my own kind, grabs my arm and tells me, in our home language to slow down. He tries to hold me back but I keep going. He says Youpas is saving our people. That somebody knows about us and so does this girl beside us.

Youpas? Was that Youpas? Off to no good no doubt or Lorpas wouldn't have run after him.

I speak in our home language, too. "I don't believe anybody but Lorpas, and I know Youpas only too well. Nothing he does is reasonable."

Is this the one called Narlpas or the one called Bolopas that I'm supposed to be looking for? Or is it another one entirely?

He won't let go. I pull him along, trying to go faster. "Anything Youpas is going to do can't be good."

"Youpas is saving our world."

"I'll bet."

I say that in the native's language. I don't know if he understands English or not.

I finally twist away and really run. Their donkey lopes along beside me. I hear the man say, "I'll bet? I'll bet? I'll bet?" as he chases after us.

LORPAS

YOUPAS RUNS STRAIGHT INTO CORWIN'S HOUSE—
runs right in and runs right out again, crosses to the
barn. . . . All this before I can catch up to him.

I'm close behind now. I go in the barn but Youpas
runs out the far side before I can grab him.

And there's Corwin, just beyond, all by himself.
He's doing Emily's job, bottle feeding the two motherless calves at the same time, a bottle in each hand.

Youpas stops. He's just standing. Looking. He has
no weapon that I know of. Thank goodness I never
bought him a hunting knife. But I've forgotten all
about. . . .

Corwin freezes. For a moment even the calves
freeze. I leap. I tackle Youpas. We're both on the
ground, but he turns around fast and then I'm in his
line of sight. Now I know the discomfort and fear of
being helpless on the other end of the freeze. No
wonder he was furious at me. But he can't let me go.
He has to keep his stare or lose me. And now
Corwin and the calves are free. I can see everything
that's going on and yet I can't move or turn my eyes
away. But nor can Youpas.

Not such a great talent when there are other
people out of the line of sight.

I see Corwin out of the corner of my eyes drop
one bottle and hit Youpas with the other. He has to
hit several times before Youpas falls back and lets
me go.

Those bottles for calves are a lot bigger than for babies but they're only plastic so Youpas isn't that hurt, but he's confused and freezing has worn him out—as it has me on the other end of it. I sit on him, careful to keep looking away.

Corwin says, "I thought you'd left," and I say, "I tried to but he . . . Hugh took over."

"He sure got cleaned up. If this really is the same man."

"The same."

But here's Allush. She squats down beside us, stares at Youpas. I suppose trying to see, is it really him, slacks, good sweater, fancy shoes. . . . And Youpas looks up at her, says, "Good God, who is it? Is it really?" while she says, more or less the same things. Then she says, "You look great," and Youpas looks away, as if ashamed. I feel him go limp.

Here come the others, including Toots. Corwin is staring at his daughter. Here she is, not in school, all dressed for traveling, and with Jack again. In fact as they came out from the backdoor of the barn, they were holding hands. As soon as Emily sees her father she lets go. Now he's really angry. And he's more worried about her than Youpas.

We're all hunkering down in the soft earth that's mostly mashed-up horseshit, but nobody seems to notice or care.

Corwin says, "I'm sending you down to Aunt May's."

"Daddy!"

"I quit. It's too hard—trying to bring up a teenage girl. You're outta here."

"Oh, Daddy!"

Nobody is paying any attention to Youpas. I'm not either. We're right at the back of the barn. There's a pitchfork leaning against the wall. Youpas pushes me off and that's what he grabs.

Now, all of us at the same time, are *really* frozen and with as much discomfort as if held by the freeze. In fact it seems a lot scarier and more dangerous than the freeze ever was. Nobody dares move.

Youpas has his back against the side of the barn. He looks back and forth at all of us, but he's clearly more wary of me than of any of the others.

I'm the one, haven't kept my promise to Corwin. I have to act before somebody gets hurt.

Then Youpas looks right at me as if he knows I'll be the one to act first. He says, "You're dead already."

Even as I leap, I know he's probably right.

ALLUSH

I'M RIGHT BEHIND LORPAS. I LEAP. I YELL. AND those other men, the one of their kind and the one of my kind are right beside me. Surely Youpas can't get all of us at the same time.

Lorpas is down.

I'm thinking, but! But it can't be. I just found him. Is he dead already?

The pitchfork is stuck in Lorpas and Youpas can't get it out in order to hit at the rest of us.

That other man, the one of my own kind, knocks him down, and away from the pitchfork. Youpas looks winded and scared. We were all banging on him long after he was down, but mostly getting in each other's way. I'd like him gone. I'd like to get out one of those homers right now and send him back to his family of important people. I'm thinking, go and be important and don't come back.

I don't want to stop beating on him but I do. He's not even defending himself anymore. I'm sitting in the dried up horseshit practically on top of him. I don't care if he lives or dies. I turn around and kneel beside Lorpas.

It's a three pronged fork. Two prongs seem stuck, just below the collarbones on each side, and the third is stuck in his shoulder. There's not much blood. I don't know if he's unconscious or dead or maybe dying. I don't dare touch him. Everyone looks

like they don't know what to do. None of us dare
pull it out.

Suddenly he takes a big breath and then cries out
in pain, though he's still unconscious. I cry out in
pain, too.

That native man tells the girl to call a doctor, and
fast. She stares at him but doesn't move. "Go! Go!"
he says, and she finally comes to and does.

Then that man says, "I don't know. I should . . . "
and then "Should I?" then, "Should I cut the handle
off? But that might hurt him worse."

Lorpas is breathing big painful breaths and crying
out at each one but he still seems to be unconscious.

The native man says, "We should try to hold it
steady." So we kneel across from each other and try
to brace the handle.

It seems a long time before the ambulance arrives.

They saw off the handle with a special little saw,
then, pitchfork end and all, they take Lorpas off to
the hospital. It's two towns down. They don't let me
go with him but that native man says he'll drive me
there right away. Then he says Emily comes, too. He
says, "From now on, I won't let her out of my sight."

I ask the man, "How long will it take? How far
is it?"

"Maybe half an hour."

"My God."

"But remember it'll take them half an hour to get
there, too, and we're not far behind. And they probably won't let you see him right away, anyway."

We get in the pickup, all of us, Youpas, too, though at first the native man wants him not to come and then he wonders what to do with him. He says he certainly doesn't want Hugh left alone here. He says, "You, whoever you are, get in."

Youpas gets up. Parts of his face are swelling and turning purple and he's limping and holding on to his arm. I hope there's something badly wrong with it. That might keep him out of trouble.

I'm disappointed. I was hoping he'd be . . . well, dead. Here he is all freshly shaven, hair cut short and nice clothes. I don't know who he is anymore. He's even looking as if he hadn't meant it to happen. Though why would anyone attack with a pitchfork if they hadn't wanted to kill somebody?

I say, "There, you have what you wanted."

I feel so much like hitting him again, I have to turn away. I should have been the one jumped first before Lorpas did. I should have made Youpas hit at me, then he might have hesitated.

"I liked Lorpas." Youpas says it as if he's surprising himself, and he said "liked" as if Lorpas is dead already.

ONLY THE NATIVE MAN AND THE GIRL RIDE IN THE cab. The rest of us ride in the back.

The bed of the pickup has straw on it and old horse blankets scattered over that.

I open my little pack of homers, each with its

insertion needle. I hand one to Youpas. I say, "Go home. I hope you like it. I didn't, but then I'm a peasant back there. You're not. Your family wants you back. You'll like it. You can be important. You own a tower."

He doesn't take it. I wonder if I can insert it when he isn't looking. Unfortunately it won't be instant. Somebody will have to come for him.

He says, "The stupid sapiens are going to find out all about us."

"And that's your fault. But you can't live your whole life not trusting anybody. Besides, like you always kept saying, they're too stupid."

"You and Mollish never felt that way."

"How would they get to our homeworld?"

"Once they know we exist they might be smart enough to figure out a way."

"You can't have it both ways, smart *and* stupid."

Then I try to talk to the other man of my own kind. I speak in the natives' language first. I'm better at that than in my own. I say I'm Allush. He shakes his head and says, I greet, in our home language. Then in English, "I no talk this talk."

I switch to Betasha. I tell him I've just come back from the homeworld and that I'm looking for somebody named Bolowpas or Narlpas.

He ducks his head the way we do when naming ourselves. (I don't, but my parents did.) Says, as my people do, "Right here is Narlpas. For here, Lorpas names me Jack."

"I have a beacon for you. If you want to go home."

He waves his hand in circles. It reminds me of that brushing-away flies motion, though this is different. He says, "I don't know. But not yet. Right here is Emily. I love her."

In our language the word he uses for love means more than just to love.

"But she's a child."

"But she loves, too."

Youpas says, "There, maybe he'll believe *you*. He doesn't believe any of us."

LORPAS

"YOU ALMOST DIED."

I hear it as if from a distance—as if through a fog.

If there ever was a reason to come to as fast as I can, that voice would be it. Someone is holding my hand. I struggle to lift myself out of the heavy layer of darkness.

Someone is saying, "Who? Who?" I realize I'm the one asking it and it's me who almost died.

I try to say, "Wake me up," but it comes out muddled.

Someone wipes my face with cold water and, finally, I do come to, and here she is, looking down at me.

I say, "Allusha."

She brings me water and a straw as if she knew it was what I wanted.

She sits beside me and holds my hand again. Leans and kisses it, says, again, "You almost died." She rests her forehead on the bed by my shoulder. I think she's crying but I don't think she wants me to know. I wish I could hold her but there's an IV in my arm.

I drift off but wake again, this time with a jerk and a shout.

She lifts her head, asks, worried, "What? What?"

I say, "Pitchforks." I want to make it a joke so as not to worry her. I try to laugh but it hurts.

I don't say anymore about it, but the image of the pitchfork just before it went into my chest is clearer than the room around me right now. To distract myself I ask, "How long has it . . . ?"

"Three days. I thought. . . . I didn't know. . . . But you're all right now."

We sit quietly. I keep dozing off but that image keeps coming back. I worry that she might leave me alone with the pitchfork. I say, "Stay."

"I won't leave. Look there, they've put up a cot for me. I said I was your wife so they let me. That native man, Corwin, helped convince them."

That pitchfork image won't go away. I want to think about other things. I want her to keep talking. "What's happening?"

"The rest have gone. Back to Corwin's. Oh, and Emily! Corwin drove her down to her aunt's. She couldn't stop crying. Then he came back to be with you. And then he took everybody back to his place."

"What about Jack then?"

"I think he understands. Maybe. I talked to him. I guess it's good he hasn't any money. First thing we know, he might be down in L.A."

"What about Youpas?"

That view of a pitchfork has Youpas' face behind it, eyes wide, mouth in an angry grin.

"He has a broken arm. They patched him up and then Corwin took him to the police."

"What! How could you let that happen?"

"We couldn't help it. But that was after. Everything's changed now."

"I guess so."

I don't have the energy to be upset. Besides, I'm too happy with Allush right here beside me.

"They wanted to give you a transfusion and they found out. . . ."

"Found out!"

"No, no. Wait. They did find out about all of us having an odd kind of blood but—and don't be angry—Youpas was the only one who could give you a transfusion. I wanted to, but he was the best match."

"But they found out."

"No, it's not what you think. They didn't find out about us being from some other planet, they just thought we had a kind of blood they'd never known about before. They're going to write us up in some journals. They're saying we're Neanderthals. They've got pictures of us in the papers already. Funny, though, some of the pictures are of just regular natives. No wonder we get along so well here. They're saying there are probably a lot of Neanderthals here that they don't know about and haven't thought of looking for until us."

We keep quiet for a while, but then I remember.

"You went . . . home."

"I thought you were right behind me."

"I would have come with you but it all happened so fast."

"I didn't like it there. And I wanted to come back because of you. Besides I was the wrong kind. I'm not sure about that, but I think I was. What kind are you? Do you know? Maybe that's why my blood was the wrong type and Youpas . . . he's the right kind . . . maybe that's why he could give you a transfusion."

"You're the right kind for me."

She leans over the bed and gives me a real kiss. Then says, "Why didn't you kiss me back when we were out in the mountains sleeping next to each other?" Then she kisses me again.

"I wasn't sure you wanted somebody who limps

and has a badly scarred face and white hair around
the edges and. . . ."

"Don't be silly."

"Does our kind marry?"

"Nobody ever said we didn't. But I'm just as
happy telling everybody we are already."

"Call it pair bond."

EPILOGUE

As soon as I'm able to leave the hospital Corwin takes us home with him. Jack and I and Allush are nominally his hired hands. I can't do much yet but they can. For now, Corwin doesn't pay us except in food and housing. Allush and I get Emily's room and Jack is back in the barn.

Allush visited Youpas in prison and inserted a homer. They snatched him home just before his trial. First thing I had my arm free of the IV, I popped out the one Allush has in her ear.

Corwin wanted us to marry the way the natives do and so we did. Actually Allush wanted to, too. Emily came up for the ceremony. She looked sad the whole time. Corwin stayed close by, not, he said, because of Jack, but because of Emily. She's the one he doesn't trust. I miss her. Of course Corwin misses her the most. He's always driving down to L.A. to see how she is. We look after things here when he's gone.

Jack is going to stay. Corwin has hired him permanently. Back on Betasha he was a peasant. I can't believe it, but Jack has made good friends with the

housekeeper and is starting to learn to cook. I don't
know if he's secretly waiting for Emily to grow up or
not. I saw them talking at the wedding. He looked
brotherly even though he held her hand. Whatever
he said, she had tears in her eyes afterwards.

I'm still doing a lot of sitting around reading—
National Geographics, *Discover* magazine and such.
When I read them I always think of Ruth.

I guess the image of the pitchfork is going to be in
my life from now on. Sometimes I lean over, looking
into a dark corner and here it comes, straight at me,
and with Youpas' wide eyed, crazy face behind it. I
gasp. I can't help it, but I'm all right.

That money Olowpas gave Allush might have
meant something fifty years ago. Ten thousand dollars. I'll give some to Corwin and I'll take some to
that house I robbed. Maybe Allush and I will be
bums, but at least we've got identities now. Even
Social Security numbers and drivers' licenses. All
that publicity helped. Everybody helped us.
Everybody was glad to find out about us—as
Neanderthals that is. I don't think they'll find
Betasha. Lucky for us they think Homo sapiens sapiens are the only primates smart enough to go from
one world to another.

I wonder if they think they've found a class of
people that can be maids and gardners and handy-
men and never aspire to anything else. If that's what
they think, Allush and I will be good examples.
That's all we aspire to, too, and glad of it.

When spring comes, Allush and I will hike up to the Secret City. If we can find it. Neither of us knows the way, but we'll fish and swim, and Allush can climb trees and make foxes and ravens into pets. Maybe it'll turn out to be a camping trip to nowhere. We don't care. If we don't find it this year, then we will the next or the next. We'll show it to our children, not as anything like the world where we came from, but as an odd, heavy, imaginary city that makes no sense at all. We'll try to keep it secret though.

DATE DUE
